THE SPANISH HAWK

There were five dead men in the cabin of the boat, and the boat was lying under six fathoms of Caribbean water. The men had not been drowned; they had been shot through the head at close range; and it was obvious that the shooting had been very recent, for the bodies were still in good condition.

John Fletcher had gone down to take photographs of a sunken ship, but he took photographs of the boat and the dead men instead. That was his first mistake. His second mistake was to talk about it to Joby Thomas, because once two people had the secret it was not a secret any more. Soon Fletcher was having trouble with the island police and with some men who belonged to President Clayton Rodgers's private army of thugs. He was also in a bit of bother with two men from the CIA; and what with one thing and another, he began to wish he had followed his first impulse and had said nothing to anyone about the boat and the dead men. Life would have been quieter and a good deal safer.

The Spanish Hawk

JAMES PATTINSON

ROBERT HALE · LONDON

© James Pattinson 1977, 2005
This edition 2005

ISBN 0 7090 7840 4

Robert Hale Limited
Clerkenwell House
Clerkenwell Green
London EC1R 0HT

2 4 6 8 10 9 7 5 3 1

Printed in Great Britain by
St Edmundsbury Press Limited, Bury St Edmunds, Suffolk.
Bound by Woolnough Bookbinding Limited.

CONTENTS

1.	Not Funny	7
2.	Leave It To Us	17
3.	Happy Dreams	29
4.	And Something On Top	45
5.	Police	59
6.	Pressing Invitation	73
7.	With Us Now	90
8.	So Many Enemies	102
9.	Night Operation	116
10.	The Right Price	129
11.	Touch Wood	143
12.	Some Girl	156
13.	Confrontation	169
14.	Of Interest	185

ONE

NOT FUNNY

The ship was lying on the bottom in ten fathoms of limpid water. She was lying on her starboard side, and her masts and funnel slanted upward at an angle of thirty degrees to the horizontal. She was a steamship of the old three-island type, a freighter of possibly five thousand tons, and it might have been imagined that she had foundered in a hurricane if it had not been for the hole in her port side where the torpedo had ripped her open.

The hole told how long she had been there: it had to be more than thirty years, because the war ended in 1945 and even before that the U-boats had drawn away from the Caribbean when the hunting in those waters became less happy.

So she had lain there for all those years and the marine creatures had made use of her as they would have made use of any natural rock formation on the floor of the sea. There were incrustations of barnacles; fishes swam in and out through the torpedo hole, exploring the engine-room as though it had been a submarine cave; shoals of them sailed like flocks of birds between the trailing strands of rigging, the airless ventilators and the silent winches, the four-inch gun at the stern and the twelve-pounder in the bows. And there she would continue to lie, this victim of man's violence, undisturbed by any convulsion on the surface, while hidden inside her were the bones of drowned or slaughtered seamen, picked clean by underwater predators and scavengers long, long ago.

Fletcher swam warily, peering through the eyepiece of his aqualung and watching for snags like jagged projections of iron or lengths of slimy cordage that might entangle the legs; watching also for sharks or barracuda, the wolves and jackals of the depths.

He swam along the sloping port side of the ship and saw the gaping hole where the torpedo had torn the life out of her that long past moonlit night, and he tried to imagine what it had been like for those on board. The sudden blast coming without warning, and then the water gushing in, the vessel sinking, the panic rush for rafts and lifeboats . . . And now it was all so calm, so silent; something that was past, finished, completed; the men no longer mourned, perhaps even forgotten.

He swam past the hole and could see the abandoned davits above it, and then he was gliding along the forepart of the hull towards the bows. He came round the forecastle and only then did he see the boat.

The boat had come down between the foremast and the centre-castle of the ship, but it had not been there so long; not by years; not by decades. Indeed, when he came closer to it Fletcher made a guess that it had not been there for more than a week or so, and maybe less. It did not have the look of something that had been lying on the bottom for any length of time; it had not yet merged with its surroundings, had not been colonised by the inhabitants of the sea bed; the paint still looked good.

It was a sea-going launch, maybe thirty feet long and ten feet in the beam. As far as Fletcher could judge, it was not of the most modern design; probably a fairly old boat that had done its share of work before ending up the way it had. And why had it finished like that? Certainly no torpedo had sent it plunging to the bottom; there were no U-boats hunting in these waters now, and a boat of that size would never have been worth the expenditure of a torpedo anyway. But there had to be a reason : boats did not sink without cause; and there had been no recent storms that might have overwhelmed such a craft. So why?

He swam in closer. The boat, unlike the ship, had settled on an even keel and was to all appearances undamaged; it might have been floating on the surface rather than resting on the bottom. There was a cockpit aft and a cabin in the forepart. The cockpit was abandoned, but whether or not the same could be said of the cabin was impossible to be sure without investigating further. Fletcher decided to investigate further.

The door of the cabin was closed, but it was neither jammed nor locked; under the pressure of Fletcher's hand it swung slowly and a shade reluctantly inward. He floated in the doorway, peering into the interior. Diffused light filtered in through the windows on either side, revealing the bodies in their various attitudes of death. He felt a sense of shock and an impulse to retreat, to get back to the surface as quickly as possible, to the fresh air and the warm sunshine. Nevertheless, he stayed there; he counted the bodies carefully and made the total five : two blacks and three whites.

Five dead men in a sunken boat! And again, why? Why all in the cabin? Had they made no attempt to escape? Had they remained there passively waiting to be drowned without so much as a struggle? Or had they perhaps not been drowned? Could there possibly be some more sinister explanation for their presence there?

He steeled himself and moved into the cabin and came to the first man. The man was lying on his back, stretched out as though sleeping; but it would be a long, long sleep for him. Fletcher took a closer look and saw the hole in the man's head where the bullet had gone in; and he did not like what he saw. He had a feeling that he had stumbled on something which it might be wiser to forget. For his own good it might be best to get out of that cabin at once and never come back, never breathe a word about what he had seen, never.

But he could not do it; he could not leave the thing like that, however much it might have been in his own interests to do so. It was just not possible.

He examined the other bodies, one by one. Each man had been shot in the head, probably at close range with a small calibre pistol. It looked like an execution rather than a fight, as though perhaps the men had been taken by surprise. But by whom? And for what reason? Who were these dead men?

Fletcher had come down with the intention of photographing an old ship sunk by a U-boat in 1942, and he had all the necessary equipment; instead, he took pictures of five dead men and the boat that was their coffin. When he left the cabin he was careful to close the door behind him. To protect the bodies? To prevent them from escaping? He himself would have found it difficult to provide an answer.

*   *   *

" You find anything?" Joby asked, helping Fletcher to take off the aqualung.

Joby Thomas was a real black Negro; six feet tall and with about as much fat on him as you would find on a wire nail. They were on board his motor-boat *Snow Queen*, and it might have been said that he was doing only what he was being paid to do; only he would have done it anyway, because he was John Fletcher's very good friend.

It was not a friendship of very long standing : about six months or so, which was the length of time Fletcher had been resident on the island, and during which time he had been lodging with the Thomases—Joby, his wife Paulina and the two kids, Willie and Millie. A few months before that Fletcher had come into a legacy on the death of an uncle; nothing very big, but enough to persuade him to pack in his job with an insurance company and pull up roots. He was twenty-five and unattached, so why not make use of the money while he could still enjoy life rather than stow it away in some bank or building society, or even in shares that might go up but could as easily slide down?

He decided to go out to the West Indies and write a book.

He had never thought of writing a book until that moment, but it seemed a good thing to do; the legacy was not going to last for ever and he would need to make some more money somehow. So why not make it by writing, which was surely as easy a way as any? After six months he had still not started on the book; there were so many other things to do and there was no hurry; he would wait for some ideas to bubble up from the subconscious, which was a well-known breeding ground for ideas, jot down a few notes, let the thing germinate. It looked like being a slow germination, but never mind; life was good; life, in fact, had never been better.

" I found a ship," he said.

Joby nodded. He was about the same age as Fletcher. Same height, too. Fletcher was of a thicker build, but there was no fat on him, either; he had big bones. Some people might have judged him at first sight to be a trifle awkward in his movements, but they would have been wrong; he was surprisingly agile and light on his feet. He had fair hair, a rather craggy face and a nose slightly bent in the middle as the result of a punch received in a boxing bout fairly early in life. He had never rated himself as handsome, and as far as he knew no one else had, either. It had never worried him.

" Told you she's somewheres around here," Joby said. " My pa, he'd talk about it plenty. Nearest the war ever come to the island. Nearest anybody ever wanted it to come, I reckon." He pointed towards a rocky islet thrusting up from the water some distance away. " Knowed it was a bit to the east of that rock."

Joby's motor-boat was not very new and not very big, but he maintained it in first-class condition. It was his chief means of livelihood; it paid the expenses of his little family, and none of them had yet gone hungry or badly clothed; which was something to be thankful for with things the way they were. Most of his income came from American holiday-makers who wanted to go fishing or skin-diving or simply for a nice quiet trip along the coast. When there were no bookings of that kind he would give Fletcher the offer of a cheap rate, sometimes little more than the cost of the fuel. He said it was better than hanging around the house doing nothing. Not that Fletcher had ever seen Joby hanging around doing nothing; he always seemed to be able to find a job to do.

"I found something else down there, too," Fletcher said.

He had not intended telling Joby; he had not intended telling anyone. Once it was told he knew that he had to become involved, and he did not wish to be involved in a thing like that. But it had slipped out, and he had a feeling that the moment he had spoken those seven innocent words he had in effect said good-bye to the quiet life and had taken a step into another kind of world—a world of violence and intrigue; a world he wanted no part in.

"Uh-huh?" Joby said; and waited.

Fletcher saw that he could still draw back. There were plenty of things he could have seen down there, apart from the ship. He could make up some story for Joby; he could destroy the film in his underwater camera; he could keep the discovery to himself and stay out of trouble. That would be the wise course; he was under no compulsion to reveal what he had seen; it was none of his business, nothing that he need get caught up with.

Nevertheless, as though under some irresistible compulsion to reveal it all, he went on.

"I found a boat."

"A boat?" Joby said. "You mean a lifeboat?"

"No, not a lifeboat. A motor-boat. Like this. Only bigger. A cabin cruiser."

"Well, now," Joby said thoughtfully. "Is that so?"

"Did you hear of any boat being sunk around here lately?"

Joby shook his head. "Not me. But mebbe it wasn't lately. Mebbe bin down there a long time."

" No; it hasn't been there long. Not more than a week or so, I'd say."

" You sure 'bout that?"

" Pretty sure."

" That's strange. Bin calm weather. No high winds. Why would a boat go down like that? Why no report about it?"

" That's what I've been wondering. There's something else I've been wondering about, too. The bodies."

Joby looked startled. " Bodies?"

" Five men. In the cabin. They've been shot."

Joby's eyes opened very wide. " Now what you sayin'? Shot? For sure?"

" For sure," Fletcher said. " One bullet each. Through the head. No sign of any struggle. It was just as if they'd been executed."

" My, oh my! And you figure it wasn't so long ago?"

" Couldn't have been. Not with the bodies still in the condition they are. Not by my reckoning."

"So!" Joby made a soft hissing noise through his pursed lips, and he was frowning a little. Fletcher wondered whether he was also thinking this might be something in which it would be advisable not to get involved. " Now what you aimin' to do 'bout it?"

" I don't know," Fletcher said.

" Could just do nothin'. Nobody goin' to know if you don' say a word."

" Is that what you're advising?"

" I don't advise nothin'," Joby said.

" But you think it might be best not to get mixed up in this thing?"

" Well, what d'you think? Five men get theirselves shot through the cranium and dumped at the bottom of the sea.

Stan's to reason there's somebody aroun' that don't much want them drug up to the surface. It's like somebody might get awful sore at anyone as put that kinda thing in motion. Like somebody might get to doin' some more shootin'. You get me?"

" Sounds to me as if you are telling me to leave it alone."

" I'm tellin' you what might be safest."

" And if I don't say anything about it, you won't, either? Is that it?"

" I di'n't see no boat," Joby said. " I di'n't see no men with holes in their heads. I jus' di'n't see nothin'. No, sir."

Which was one way of saying that if Fletcher decided to keep his mouth shut, Joby would do the same. But would it work out like that? A secret held by more than one person was no longer a secret. Suppose Joby were to tell his wife, not meaning it to go any further. Would Paulina be able to keep such an exciting piece of information to herself? He doubted it. No; the thing had to come out now, and it would be better to reveal it at once than to let it leak out gradually; that way matters would only be so much the worse.

Joby had been watching him closely and appeared to have read his thoughts. " Ain't going to leave it, are you? Ain't jus' goin' to forget all about it."

" I don't think it's possible," Fletcher said. " For one thing, it'd be committing an offence not to report it. And then if it did leak out we'd be in worse trouble."

" How you reckon it could leak out?"

" Well, things do, you know."

Joby understood. " Okay. Mebbe you're right. So you tell the cops, huh?"

" I think I'll have to. Then it'll be for them to figure it

out. Anyway, what can happen to me if I tell them? I didn't shoot the men and sink the boat. Nobody's going to say I did. I'm clean."

" You're clean sure enough," Joby admitted. " But bein' clean don' mean there ain't nothin' can happen to you all the same. Mebbe you's okay with the cops an' mebbe not so okay with some other people."

" You're trying to discourage me."

" I'm lookin' at things the way they are."

" It still adds up to a lot of plain discouragement."

" An' you still aim to go an' tell the cops?"

" I still aim to do that," Fletcher said.

Joby shrugged resignedly. "Okay then. We may as well head for home."

TWO

LEAVE IT TO US

Joby took his boat up to a pier on the east side of James-town harbour and said he would wait there until Fletcher had completed his business with the police. It was then mid-afternoon and the town was sweltering in the sun; white walls reflecting the glare, tarmac softening in the heat, an odour of petrol exhaust and ripe fruit hanging in the air.

It was a ten-minute walk from the waterfront to police headquarters, a plain, architecturally undistinguished, four-storey building with a large car-park in front and a few palm-trees giving a bit of shade here and there. Fletcher walked across the car-park and up the steps to the main entrance. He had never previously been inside the place and he was not at all sure he ever wanted to be inside it again; it made him nervous. Perfectly innocent though he knew himself to be, in these surroundings he could not avoid a sense of guilt; it was almost as though he had come to confess to a crime rather than to report one committed by someone else, some person or persons unknown.

There was a counter on the right of the entrance hall, with a couple of policemen behind it hammering laboriously away at typewriters and another one, with sergeant's stripes on his sleeves, using a telephone. They were all black and looked well fed; they were wearing short-sleeved green shirts and green trousers, and they had leather belts with holstered revolvers and handcuffs attached to them. The fact that the island police was an armed force gave Fletcher no feeling of confidence at all; he had a grave suspicion of all armed police. Though if it came to the point, practically all the police in the world were armed except the British; and the way things were going, even they might be compelled to come to it before so very much longer. There was violence everywhere, and how else could you deal with the armed criminal than by taking up arms also?

He went over to the counter and waited patiently while the sergeant finished his telephone conversation, and tried not to look like a criminal.

"Yeah," the sergeant said; "sure we'll do that. That's what we're here for . . . No; no need to worry . . . Well, I can't promise that; now how could I? We're not supermen . . . You thought we were? That's nice." He chuckled cosily, enjoying the joke with whoever it was on the other end of the line, and there was still some of the smile remaining on his face when he put the telephone down and turned to deal with Fletcher.

"Some guys," he said, "they think we can work miracles. Get their car stolen in the morning; expect it back as good as new so's they can drive out to Mariana Bay for the evening. Supermen!" He gave another chuckle, then cut it off abruptly. "Yes, sir; and what can we do for you?"

"I want to report a sunken boat," Fletcher said.

The sergeant gave him a long, hard look. Then he said slowly, as if to get the matter entirely clear: "You want to report a sunken boat?"

" And a killing."

" And a killing?" The sergeant was not smiling now. He looked as if he had never smiled in his life.

" Five killings," Fletcher said.

The sergeant was frowning. The two typewriters had stopped clattering. The two other policemen had turned on their chairs and were looking at Fletcher.

" Five?"

" Yes," Fletcher said. " Five men shot through the head."

The sergeant gave a sigh; the sigh of a man who feels that his patience is being sorely tried. " And where are these five men who've been shot through the head?"

" In the sunken boat."

" You saw them?"

" Yes."

" What were you doing when you saw them?"

" Skin-diving."

" Where?"

" To the east of the island; a few miles out. I was looking for an old ship that was torpedoed in the last war."

It was apparent that the sergeant knew about the ship. For the first time since the start of the conversation he ceased to give the impression of someone who believed that he was dealing with a lunatic.

" Did you find the ship?"

" Yes."

" And a boat, too?"

" Yes. The boat was lying on the bottom with the ship, but it hadn't been there long. The dead men were all in the cabin."

" But you don't think they'd been drowned?"

" Not unless somebody shot them afterwards."

" And you don't think that's likely?"

" Do you?"

" No," the sergeant said; " I don't." He gave Fletcher another long, hard look, as though trying to make up his mind as to whether or not he was being told a cock-and-bull story; then he said : " Wait here. I'll be back in a minute."

He came out from behind the counter and walked away down a corridor. Fletcher waited. The two other policemen had not yet started again on their typing; they were still looking at him. He knew that if he made any kind of move to leave the building they would be on to him like a flash. He made no move; he just stood there feeling uncomfortable and hoping that the sergeant would soon come back.

In fact it was less than a minute that he had to wait. The sergeant returned accompanied by an older man with three stars on his shoulder straps. This man was thinner and his hair was beginning to go grey. He had a disillusioned air, as though he no longer expected anything good to come to him, and least of all from Fletcher. He introduced himself as Captain Green and began by getting Fletcher's name for the record; which was something the sergeant had omitted to do.

" I take it that you're here on holiday, Mr. Fletcher?"

" Not exactly," Fletcher said. " I'm here to write a book." He saw the captain's head give a slight jerk and his eyes narrowed a shade, as though he had heard an incriminating admission. Perhaps it had been an unwise thing to say. " I'm lodging with Mr. and Mrs. Joby Thomas in Port Morgan."

" And you've found five dead men?"

" Yes."

" You'd better come into this room over here and tell me all about it, if you don't mind, Mr. Fletcher."

" I don't mind," Fletcher said. " That's what I'm here for."

The sergeant came with them. It was a plain square room with a table and two chairs. Fletcher sat on one chair and the captain sat on the other, facing him across the table. The sergeant stood by the door. Fletcher felt more like a criminal under interrogation every minute.

" Now," Captain Green said, " let's have it from the beginning. All of it."

Fletcher gave him all of it from the beginning. The captain listened intently, putting in a question now and then. Fletcher told him everything except the bit about taking photographs of the dead men and the boat. He could not have said why he omitted that part, but he did.

When he had finished Captain Green sat for a while in silence, as if turning it all over in his own mind. Then he got up suddenly, pushing the chair noisily back and nearly oversetting it.

" Wait here," he said. It seemed to be one of the favoured orders. They all seemed to think that, given half a chance, Fletcher would run away and never come back. Which was rather ridiculous really, seeing that he had come there entirely voluntarily.

" Don't worry," he said. " I'll wait." But in fact he was the one who was beginning to worry. He could not have explained why; it was just a feeling he had, a feeling that he was indeed becoming involved in something he might have been well advised not to become involved in; something which could have a far deeper significance than he or Joby had supposed. Maybe he ought to have paid more heed to that first instinct to keep his mouth firmly shut. But it was too late now; he had opened it and the wheels had been set in motion.

Captain Green left the sergeant to keep an eye on him and make sure that he really did wait there. Whether he accepted Fletcher's word or not, he was taking no chances. The sergeant stayed by the door, saying nothing. Fletcher shifted uneasily on his chair and tried to think of something to say, because the silence was getting on his nerves. But nothing came up: the sergeant and he had nothing in common, nothing to discuss, except possibly the subject of mass homicide.

Finally he cleared his throat and said: " Do you know where he's gone?"

" No," the sergeant said.

Which effectively put an end to that conversation.

Some five or ten minutes had passed when the door opened again and Captain Green came in.

He said: " Colonel Vincent would like to see you, Mr. Fletcher. If you'll just come with me."

Fletcher, reflecting that he seemed to be making a rapid rise through the ranks of the police and that the information he had brought was undoubtedly being treated as a matter of importance, got up and followed Captain Green out of the room. The captain led the way along a corridor, up a flight of concrete stairs, and along another corridor until they came to a door marked in gilt lettering: " Colonel Arthur W. Vincent." Captain Green tapped lightly on the door with his knuckles, a voice on the other side mumbled something that might have been an invitation to enter, and they went in. Green closed the door gently behind them.

" Mr. Fletcher, sir."

It was a fairly large room with a lot of window space along one side. There were some solid chairs and a solid mahogany desk and a street map of Jamestown hanging on the wall on the right. There were some red-topped pins stuck in the map at various points, which might have been marking the scenes of crimes or trouble spots, or anything else if it came to that.

Colonel Arthur W. Vincent was sitting at the desk with a pen in his hand and a sheaf of papers in front of him. He was a little dried-up strip of a man with skin the colour of cold ashes. He did not look like a high-ranking police officer; he was wearing a rumpled brown cotton suit and he looked more like an office clerk or possibly the proprietor of a fifth-rate used-car saleyard. He had the keen, calculating, slightly shifty eye of a used-car salesman, and Fletcher's immediate impression was that Colonel Vincent was not a man he would have trusted with half an ounce of boiled sweets—or fourteen grammes if you were using the metric system of weights and measures.

" Ah!" Vincent said; and he gave a smile that revealed some gold fillings in his teeth and looked about as genuine as a bottle of Japanese Scotch whisky. " So you are Mr. Fletcher. Please sit down." He flipped a couple of bony fingers in the general direction of one of the solid chairs, and Fletcher walked over to it and sat down. Captain Green remained standing.

" I understand," Vincent said, " that you came to report finding a sunken boat."

" And five dead men."

" Yes." There was a sibilant hiss as Vincent spoke the word, as though he had held on to the final letter as long as possible, reluctant to let it escape. " Five men shot through the head. Is that correct?"

" It is."

Vincent was playing with the pen, setting it up on end, allowing it to fall almost to the desk, and then catching it just before it could do so. It was rather like a cat playing with a mouse.

" Mr. Fletcher," he said, " why were you diving out there? In that particular place."

" I told the captain—"

" And now I should like you to tell me. You don't mind?"

" Why should I mind?"

" Exactly. Why should you?"

" I was looking for the ship."

" Oh, the ship. Yes, of course. And you found the ship, and the boat was there also?"

" Yes."

" Why did you want to find the ship?"

" No particular reason. Just curiosity; nothing more."

" You had been told about it?"

" Yes, of course. How else would I have known it was there?"

" How else indeed. And who told you?"

" Mr. Thomas."

" Mr. Thomas, with whom you are lodging?" Colonel Vincent was very correct in his grammar.

" Yes."

" And it was Mr. Thomas who took you out in his boat?"

" It was."

" Do you do much skin-diving, Mr. Fletcher?"

" I don't know what you'd call much. I do a fair amount of it."

" I understand you are a writer," Vincent said.

" Well, yes, I am." Fletcher failed to see the point of all these questions. What possible bearing could such personal details have on the matter of the five dead men in the sunken boat? " But I don't see——"

" Had the search for the ship anything to do with your writing?"

" No, not really."

" This book that you told Captain Green you came here to write—what is it about?"

" I don't know."

Vincent let the pen fall and trapped it under his right hand as though arresting it in the act. " You don't know?"

Fletcher was faintly embarrassed. " That is to say, I haven't actually started on it yet. I'm still casting about for a subject."

" And how long have you been here?"

" About six months."

" Six months and you still haven't found a subject! Isn't that taking rather a long time?"

" Perhaps. But I still don't see what this has to do with——"

" What kind of a writer are you, Mr. Fletcher?"

" How do you mean—what kind?"

Vincent picked up the pen and rolled it between his fingers. " I mean would you, for instance, describe yourself as a political writer?"

Fletcher began to see what Vincent was getting at. But he still could not see why. Why should his political views have any bearing on the subject of the five dead men?

"The fact is," he said, "I'm not really a writer at all. That is, not yet. I mean I haven't written anything so far. Nothing that's been published."

Colonel Vincent looked as though he found that rather hard to believe. "Are you telling me that it's not your profession?"

"Not at the moment. It could be—some time in the future. You understand?"

"So what do you do for a living?"

"Nothing just now. I had some money left me."

"Very nice," Vincent said, a trifle sardonically. "That sounds an easy kind of life. It must have been a lot of money."

"Not as much as you might think. I may have to start looking for a job before very long."

"You should get on with writing that book, Mr. Fletcher," Vincent said.

Fletcher nodded. "I might just do that. After all, I've got something to write about now, haven't I?"

Vincent gave him a sharp look. "What do you mean by that?"

"Five men shot through the head, all together in the cabin of a motor-boat ten fathoms down. That's a good basis for a plot, wouldn't you say?"

"Mr. Fletcher," Vincent said, "let me give you a word of advice. Leave that plot alone. Touch that and you could be in trouble. It's not your business; it's ours. Leave it to us. Don't you think that would be best?"

"Perhaps so. It was just a thought."

"Let it stay just a thought."

"Are you warning me?" Fletcher asked.

Vincent smiled, and there were those gold-filled teeth

flashing again like danger signals. " I'm advising you—as a friend."

Fletcher reflected that if he ever became so short of friends he needed Colonel Arthur W. Vincent for one, he would really be down to the bedrock; but he did not say so, did not even hint as much; because Vincent might have been offended, and the last thing he wanted to do was to give offence to this little man with his ash-grey face and his probing eyes. Vincent as a friend might not be all that was to be desired, but as an enemy he could be deadly poison.

" In that case," he said, " I'll take the advice."

" That would be wise."

" Are you going to fish the bodies up?"

" We'll do all that is necessary. Don't worry; you've done your part and now we'll do ours."

" You don't want me any more, then?"

" If we do we'll get in touch."

It seemed to be the end of the interview. Fletcher stood up.

" By the way," Vincent said, " you didn't get a look at the name on the boat, I suppose?"

Fletcher paused. " Well, yes, as a matter of fact I did. It was rather a funny name."

" Funny?"

" Unusual."

" Ah!"

" It was *Halcón Español*, which I believe means ' Spanish Hawk '."

" Yes," Vincent said, " that is unusual. But I should not have called it funny. No, certainly not funny. Good-bye, Mr. Fletcher. And don't talk about this."

" Who would I talk to?" Fletcher said.

Vincent nodded. " Ah, who indeed !"

Fletcher left the building wondering just why Colonel Vincent should have found the name of the boat unusual but certainly not funny, and why he should have thought it necessary to give that warning not to talk about it.

But no answers floated to the surface.

THREE

HAPPY DREAMS

Joby was dozing in his boat when Fletcher got back to the pier, but he woke up quickly as Fletcher stepped down into the cockpit.

" Began to think they'd arrested you."

" I had that feeling myself once or twice."

" So what's happening?"

" I'm leaving it to them. A man named Arthur W. Vincent has it in hand. He's a colonel of police."

" I know," Joby said.

Fletcher was surprised. " You know him?"

" Not personally," Joby said. " I know about him; everybody in Jamestown does. He's Clayton Rodgers's right hand man, and there's some that say he's a bigger bastard than Rodgers himself. Though personally I'd need to have proof of that before I'd believe it possible."

Fletcher was even more surprised. He had never heard Joby quite so outspoken on the subject of President Clayton Rodgers, and it was the kind of talk that could make bad trouble for the speaker if ever it got to the wrong ears. So it just showed how much Joby had come to trust him.

It was, of course, no news to Fletcher that there were plenty of people on the island who would have been only too pleased to see President Rodgers in his coffin, and there were probably a lot who would have been perfectly willing to put him there if only they could have got near enough to him to do something about it. But Rodgers was not an easy man to assassinate; he had the power that goes with absolute rule and complete control of the police. He also had his own private army of thugs known as the Leopards.

Clayton Rodgers was a big, fat, jovial man of forty who had studied law in the United States. He had come to power by a clever manipulation of the ballot box, which had finally left the democratic machinery in a desperately run-down condition and the President firmly established as a highly autocratic head of state. In office he had continued to consolidate his position with considerable backing from the U.S. Treasury, the flow of dollars from which had been skilfully guided into those channels most favoured by the President himself and which critics considered not altogether to the benefit of the islanders as a whole.

It was said moreover that the C.I.A. kept a sharp eye on affairs and were happy to lend support to President Rodgers for fear that if he should fall the alternative might be communism on the Cuban model. To the C.I.A. virtual dictatorship by a right-wing head of state was infinitely preferable to a left-wing government, however benevolent. And of course there were many who benefited from the existing state of things. Tourists—mainly Americans—were a rich source of income; and tourists had an unfortunate habit of avoiding places where the political climate was unsettled and shots were likely to be fired in the streets. Those who made money out of the tourist industry didn't, as a general rule, give a damn what happened to those others who were out of work and near starvation. Joby Thomas himself of course profited from the American visitors, but apparently this fact did not make him an uncritical supporter of the President.

He started the engine and got the boat moving away from the pier and out into the bay. The shores of the bay were shaped like a horseshoe, with Jamestown on the inner curve. Port Morgan, where Joby lived, was near the tip of the eastern prong of the horseshoe and had once been a haunt of buccaneers, and later a naval dockyard. It had been prosperous in those days, but there were no buccaneers now and the dockyard was quietly decaying, as indeed the whole place seemed to be.

From Jamestown to Port Morgan across the bay was a distance of about a mile and a half, but by road, round the curve of the shore, it was nearly three times as far. People who did not own cars—and that included the greater part of the Port Morgan population—used the ferry whenever they wished to visit Jamestown; it cost a little more than walking but it was far less tiring.

On the trip back to base *Snow Queen* passed a cruise liner coming in. Passengers lining the rails waved a greeting; Fletcher and Joby waved back.

" More visitors for the Island Paradise," Fletcher said. It was the term they used in the travel brochures.

Joby grunted. " Paradise for some. Hell for others."

" Well, at least you're making out none too badly."

" That's true," Joby said. " But I know lots that don't do so good."

" And you think things could be better?"

" I know they could. There's a bag of money not bein' used the way it ought to be. There's a pack of people in high places linin' their pockets and sayin' to hell with the poor guys."

" And Clayton Rodgers is one of them?"

" Clayton Rodgers is the chief one. He's sittin' on top of the whole rotten system. This here island's just a playground for the rich and idle that come here to have a good time. The way things are goin', we'll soon be nothin' but a gang of waiters an' pimps an' beggars—mostly beggars."

" Now hold on, Joby. That's putting it a bit strong."

" Not too strong, it ain't."

" I've never heard you sounding off like this before."

" Mebbe 'cause I don' often let go. Mos' times I keep it bottled up. Sometimes you gotta take the cork out."

" And in your book I suppose I rate as one of the rich and idle?"

Joby gave a sudden grin, as though the dark mood had been thrust aside. " I never said that. I wouldn't call you a real rich guy; you'd be livin' it up in one of them fancy hotels if you was. Mebbe a bit idle sure enough, but you'll get over that, I guess."

" When the money's gone?"

" Yeah, when the money's gone. What you plannin' to do then?"

" There's the book."

" You ain't never started on no book yet. You think you'll ever make a livin' that way? Honest now, do you?"

" No," Fletcher said; " to be perfectly honest, I don't. But it's a nice dream."

" Nobody ever got rich dreamin'," Joby said. " Not as I recall."

The boat chugged on across the bay. Behind them was Jamestown, and beyond Jamestown the hills were green with vegetation. It was a fertile island set in a warm blue sea; it should have been, as the advertisements described it, a paradise; but, as Joby had said, it was a paradise only for some—for the tourists who came with money in their pockets and for the lucky few who grabbed that money. For those who lived in the shanty towns in homes made from old packing-cases, flattened-out oil-drums, rusty corrugated iron and tarred paper, with only the most primitive of sanitation and drainage, and perhaps a long walk to fetch water from a stand-pipe, there was little enough hint of paradise.

" Some day somebody's gotta do somethin'," Joby said. " Some day."

They came up to the Port Morgan jetty, which seemed to be in some need of repair; a lot of the timbers were rotting and the whole structure was leaning slightly to one side, as though it had been given a strong push from which it had never recovered. Away on the left were the crumbling buildings of the old dockyard, weeds growing through the broken concrete and the tendrils of creepers winding themselves round the cracked pillars and rusting iron. On the right was the wide sweep of the headland, the silvery white sand and the fringe of palm-trees, all bending in one direction like spectators at a football match trying to get a sight of the ball.

There were some kids on the jetty; it was a favourite place for kids: you could watch the ships come in; you could fish; you could make chalk marks on the boards and play intricate children's games. They were not really supposed to be there, but if they were driven away they came back; in the end nobody bothered to drive them away any more.

Fletcher and Joby pushed their way through the crowd, Fletcher carrying his camera and part of the skin-diving gear, Joby carrying the rest. Joby's bungalow was about a quarter of a mile from the jetty. There was a drainage ditch in front of it, and you had to go over a footbridge made of two planks and then along ten yards of pathway with bushes growing on each side. There was a bit of garden at the back with a rough fence round it, and there were yams and sweet corn and melons, some small orange trees and a couple of coconut palms with a hammock slung between them. The bungalow was nothing much; it had been built with sections of an old army hut, and it had a tarred felt roof which Joby had to keep patching because the rain would find a way in. But even at that it was better than most of the dwellings in Port Morgan, and it had running water and electricity, besides being large enough to provide a room for Fletcher without overcrowding the family.

Joby's children, Willie and Millie, who were four-year-old twins, came running to meet him, and they had to be picked up and made a fuss of both by Joby and Fletcher before either of the men could go into the house. Paulina was in the kitchen preparing a meal. She was really beautiful, and Fletcher had told Joby so on more than one occasion. It pleased Joby to hear compliments about his wife, and Fletcher believed that he had relayed the remarks to Paulina herself : it could have been why she was always so pleasant towards him; or maybe that was just her nature.

Joby took two cans of beer out of the refrigerator, which was one of the few luxuries in the house. At least Joby called it a luxury, though in that climate it might have been considered a necessity. He opened the cans and handed one to Fletcher.

" You could have glasses," Paulina said. " They're free."

" No need," Joby said. " Tastes better from the can."

She looked at Fletcher. " You find what you were looking for out there ?"

" Yes," Fletcher said; " we found it."

" Found somethin' else besides," Joby said.

Fletcher remembered Vincent's warning not to talk about it, but what the hell; Joby was bound to tell Paulina anyway. The twins had gone out into the garden and were playing with the hammock; he could see them from the kitchen window.

" There was a boat," he said.

Paulina listened to the story and he could see that she was worried by it.

" I wish you hadn't found it," she said.

Joby gave a laugh, making light of the matter. " Now you're goin' to say it's unlucky. I know."

" It could be. A thing like that; it's best not to get mixed up in it."

" We're not mixed up in it," Fletcher said. But he knew they were.

She knew it too. " You have to be mixed up in it if you found the bodies. And who killed them? Who were they? Why were they killed ?"

" That's for the police to find out."

The mention of the police hardly seemed to reassure her. " I wish you hadn't told them. Nobody need have known. Nobody saw you diving, did they ?"

" No."

" Then you didn't have to tell anybody. Who would have known ?"

" That's what I told him," Joby said.

Paulina shot a swift glance at him. " So you think he

shouldn't have gone to the police? You think that, too?"

Joby looked uncomfortable. " Well, I'm not sayin' that."

" You don't have to. I know."

" Anyway," Fletcher told her, " there's no need for you to worry about it. If there's going to be any trouble, I'm the one who'll be involved. I'm the one who found the boat. But why should there be trouble? All I've done is report a crime. I'm in the clear."

" Maybe it's not enough to be in the clear. Not when you're standing so close. I still say I wish you hadn't found the boat."

" Well, it's done now."

" Yes," she said; " it's done now. All we can do is hope nothing bad comes from it."

" Nothing will," Fletcher said. But he was not feeling very confident about it; in fact he was not feeling confident at all.

*   *   *

In the evening he went to see Dharam Singh. Dharam Singh and his family, which consisted of his wife, his five children, his sister and his widowed mother-in-law, occupied the ground floor of a house in what might have been described as the main street of Port Morgan. It was an old house and had been built in more prosperous times. It had a shabby grandeur, like an aristocrat who had come down in the world; there were chipped Doric pillars supporting the porch, rusty iron balconies attached to the upper windows and cracked stucco on the walls. If you looked closely at the roof you could see where one or two tiles were missing and the guttering had fallen away.

The upper floor was let to three sisters who earned a

living in ways that Dharam Singh chose not to mention. It was a condition of the agreement, so Fletcher gathered from what Singh had told him, that the sisters should never use the front door, but should gain access to their rooms by way of a back staircase which came down into the kitchen. The result of this arrangement was that, especially in the evening, there was a fairly constant stream of male visitors passing through the kitchen and up the back stairs. Mrs. Singh ignored them; if she had work to do in the kitchen she got on with it and responded to any friendly greeting on the part of a visitor with nothing more than a frigid glance, as if to indicate that she had no connection whatever with the ladies overhead.

Dharam Singh was a photographer, a small thin man with liquid brown eyes and an ingratiating smile. He did a small amount of business in Port Morgan, but earned more as a roving cameraman and freelance contributor to newspapers and magazines in various countries. He seemed to have a nose for the newsworthy event and an undoubted eye for a good picture. With his professional earnings and the rent for the upper floor, which was always promptly paid, he appeared to be managing very nicely in spite of the size of the family he had to support.

It was about eight o'clock when Fletcher arrived at Dharam Singh's house, and the street was only poorly lighted by an electric standard lamp here and there. As Fletcher stood under the porch and gave a pull on the iron handle that operated a bell inside the house he caught a glimpse of a man slipping down the alleyway which led to the back door. The upper windows were brightly outlined against the darkness of the wall and he could hear the sound of music of the pop variety, from which he gathered that the sisters' tastes in that line were strictly non-classical.

The door was opened by Dharam Singh himself, and immediately he recognised Fletcher his face creased into a smile of welcome.

" Mr. Fletcher. Ah, do step inside. So happy to see you, my dear sir."

Fletcher walked in and Dharam Singh closed the door. There was a large tiled hall from which rose the staircase that was never used, and one small electric bulb burned in the centre of an ornate glass chandelier suspended from the high ceiling. Dharam Singh stood rubbing his hands together, the thin brown fingers making a faint rasping sound like dry twigs which might at any moment burst into flame.

" And what, Mr. Fletcher sir, can I do for you?"

Fletcher pulled from his pocket the exposed film he had taken from the underwater camera.

" I should like to have this developed."

Dharam Singh took the film. " Of course. At once. All else shall wait."

" And three prints of each negative."

Dharam Singh gave a small bow. " Certainly."

Fletcher wondered whether to advise Dharam Singh to be discreet, but decided that it was unnecessary. The photographer was not likely to talk about work he did for a customer; that was hardly the way to attract further business. And Singh was above all else a businessman.

" If I call in tomorrow?"

" The prints will be ready. Never fear."

The music from the upper floor was faintly audible. Dharam Singh ignored it, pretending that it did not exist. Fletcher turned to go.

Dharam Singh said : " You would care for some refreshment perhaps?"

" Thank you," Fletcher said, " but no, not just now."

The refreshment would have been tea, and there would have been Dharam Singh's conversation. He did not feel a desire for either at that moment.

Dharam Singh nodded. " As you wish. Another time perhaps."

" Yes; another time."

Though he had not accepted Singh's offer of refreshment, Fletcher decided nevertheless to call in at another establishment which went under the name of the Treasure Ship before returning to Joby Thomas's house. The Treasure Ship could hardly have been said to live up to the splendour of its title, for it was an ill-lit, rather dingy saloon with swing half-doors, a zinc-topped counter on the left as you went in, a sanded floor and a dozen or so round tables with two or three chairs to each. It seemed, as usual, to be doing reasonably good business, but there were a few vacant tables and some space at the bar. Tobacco smoke hung like a thin fog in the motionless air, and a powerful odour of rum greeted him as he pushed his way through the swing-doors. Some of the male and female customers glanced at him as he walked in, but with no especial interest; he had been living in Port Morgan long enough to have become an accepted part of the local scene.

He ordered a beer and Fat Annie got it for him, smiling a welcome.

" You had a good day, Mist' Fletcher?"

" Good enough, Annie."

She was so wide Fletcher doubted whether she would have been able to sit in an armchair unless it had been specially made for her. So perhaps she used a settee when she wanted to relax. She was a motherly kind of person— at least she had always appeared so to him—but he had heard that she kept a machete under the counter and was quite prepared to use it if anyone caused trouble. He had never seen her use it, or even threaten to, but if it came to that he had never seen anyone cause trouble, so it could have been true.

He leaned on the bar and drank some of the beer, and he caught sight of one of the sisters who occupied the upper floor of Dharam Singh's house sitting at one of the tables with a blond-headed man who had the look of a Scandinavian seaman. He had, too, the look of a man who had progressed a considerable distance along the road to being drunk, and Fletcher thought it was high time the sister got him out of there, since he might well be the sort who would become rowdy and force Annie to bring out the machete. The sister was a well-built girl and not at all bad-looking; as in fact all three of them were, so it was easy to see why they made a fairly comfortable living and never got behind with the rent.

And then he heard Fat Annie say something that sounded like " Oh, oh !", and he saw the two men walk in, setting the doors swinging violently. They had a kind of swagger about them, an air that seemed to say they were the boss men and nobody had better get in their way. They were as lean as whipcord and as black as tar, and they had hair cut down so close you could see the scalp shining through. They were wearing suits of an exaggerated cut and startling hue, brilliantly patterned shirts, gold ear-rings and pointed shoes. They paused just inside the doorway and glanced round the room in a supercilious manner, letting their gaze rest for a moment on each person in turn before moving on to the next.

"Oh, oh!" Annie muttered again. "Leopards!"

Everything had gone very quiet. Everyone had stopped talking, stopped doing anything, as though a sudden frost had crept into the hot room. Everyone except the blond seaman; he just went on talking, and because it was all so quiet everyone could hear what he was saying. Not that it amounted to much; it was not something you would have bothered to record on tape for the benefit of posterity. It was all a bit slurred and it had to do with personal relations between himself and the sister; nothing for anyone else to bother about.

But it seemed to bother the Leopards. Possibly they thought that everyone should have closed up when they walked in—and that included the blond seaman. Possibly they thought it was an affront to their dignity that he should go on talking without their permission. Or possibly they simply resented the fact of a white man saying things like that to a black girl.

Whatever the reason, they walked across to the table where the sister and the blond seaman were sitting, and there was that swagger in their gait as if they owned the earth and meant to keep it that way. The sister saw them coming and looked scared, but the seaman was not giving a damn.

"Oh, oh!" Annie muttered a third time; and Fletcher guessed that she could see trouble coming, but she made no move to get the machete; she seemed to know that this was something out of her league, something too big for her to handle.

The Leopards reached the table, and one stood on one

side of it and one on the other. The blond seaman looked up at them. He was startled but not scared.

"What you want?" he said. "What in hell you want, huh?"

"Out!" one of the Leopards said. He gave a jerk of his left thumb in the direction of the door. "Out!"

"What the hell!" the seaman said. "What the blutty hell!"

"Out!"

The sister was standing up. "Come along. Let's go." She was scared sure enough.

"Damn that," the seaman said. "I wanna 'nother drink." His gaze swivelled round and settled on the Leopard who had told him to get out. "An' damn you too, you black bastard."

They took him then. They got his arms up behind his back, and the chair went sliding away and the table went over and there was a lot of broken glass lying on the floor. He was a big man and he looked powerful, but he didn't stand a chance; they marched him down the room and went out through the swing-doors. The sister followed, still looking scared. Fletcher thought she had some reason to be.

The Leopards came back five minutes later and the room was still silent. They walked to the bar, and Fletcher glanced at their shoes to see whether there was any blood on the pointed toes, but there was not. Maybe they had wiped it off on the seaman's clothes. They ordered rum and Annie served it to them, but no money changed hands. They were standing close to Fletcher, and the one who was the closer said:

"Who are you, whitey?"

Fletcher told him—politely.

Annie said quickly, as if scenting more trouble and wanting to head it off : " Mist' Fletcher's okay. He live here. He bin here long, long time."

" That so?" the Leopard said. He looked Fletcher slowly up and down—arrogantly, insolently. " That really so?"

" That's so," Fletcher said; still polite.

" You like it here? You like the climate mebbe? You like the people?"

" The climate's fine. The people too."

" You never wanna go back home?"

" Not yet."

" Mebbe you ain't got no home to go to." The Leopard laughed. The other Leopard laughed too. Annie appeared to relax a little; if they could laugh the crisis was perhaps over.

" Maybe I haven't," Fletcher said, playing it cool.

They seemed to lose interest in him. They drank their rum and left; they were evidently not going to make a night of it—not there. Possibly they had other business to attend to.

When they had gone the atmosphere became less tense; conversation started up again, became louder, the laughter less restrained. The Leopards had had an inhibiting effect. Annie looked as though she would have liked to spit if she had not been too much of a lady.

" Trash," she said. " Garbage scraped up off the streets of Jamestown. They got guns, too. You see them, Mist' Fletcher?"

" No," Fletcher said; " I didn't see any guns."

" Under them fancy jackets. They got guns shuh nuff. They'd use 'em too—and get away with it. Get away with murder, them Leopards. Mebbe already have."

Fletcher gathered that she did not much care for Leopards. He had never yet heard of anyone who did.

He finished his drink and walked out of the Treasure Ship, and they were still there, sitting in a car parked about fifty yards down the street. He had to pass the car and he saw that they were smoking cigars. There was no sign of the sister or the blond seaman, so maybe she had managed to get him to Dharam Singh's house. One of the Leopards stretched out an arm and knocked ash off his cigar at Fletcher's feet as he drew level with the car.

" Good night, Mr. Fletcher," he said. " Sleep well. Happy dreams."

He could hear them both laughing as he walked on. If he dreamed of them the dreams were not likely to be very happy; that was for sure.

FOUR

AND SOMETHING ON TOP

Fletcher called at Dharam Singh's house early in the morning to make sure of catching the photographer before he set out on whatever project he might have in view for that particular day. By daylight the house looked even more run down than it had in the less revealing light of the previous evening; the sun, already hot, showed up the blemishes like the wrinkles and blotches on the face of an ageing courtesan. He noticed that the curtains were still drawn across the upper windows, and was not surprised; the sisters were unlikely to be early risers. He wondered what had happened to the blond seaman; no doubt the man would eventually find his way back to his ship, rather stiff and sore and a good deal poorer. But that was no business of his.

Dharam Singh took him into what he called his studio, which was just another room with a sink in it where he did his photographic processing and took portraits if anyone happened to want something in that line.

" You've finished the pictures?"

Dharam Singh nodded. " Oh, yes, certainly. All finished."

" And they came out all right?"

" Perfectly. You are becoming quite skilful at that

kind of work, Mr. Fletcher, my good sir; really quite skilful."

" Thank you for the compliment. I'm not a professional, of course."

" A professional could hardly have done it better. Bearing in mind the circumstances, the detail is surprisingly excellent Yes, most surprisingly excellent."

Fletcher was aware that Dharam Singh was burning to ask questions about the photographs. But mixed with the curiosity there was also a certain uneasiness in his manner; perhaps a trace of shiftiness too.

" You would like to know, of course, where I took the photographs."

Dharam Singh squirmed a little. " It is not my business. Nevertheless—"

" No; it is not your business. It is the business of the police."

" The police! Are you telling me they know?"

" You don't imagine I'd keep a thing like that to myself, do you? That I would fail to report it."

" No, most certainly not. It would not be right; it would not be legal; it would not be—safe. And what will the police do now?"

" That's up to them. I suppose they'll fish up the bodies. Perhaps the boat as well."

" Yes; yes, I suppose so. And where—"

" Where is the boat? I don't think I'd better tell you that. I've had strict instructions not to talk about it."

" Ah, I understand. It might hinder investigations per- haps. And the police, they know of course about the photographs?"

" Well, as a matter of fact, no," Fletcher admitted. " I

rather think that if I had told them about those I wouldn't have been able to bring the film to you."

"That is certainly possible. But when they find out that you have taken these photographs don't you think perhaps they will be annoyed with you, Mr. Fletcher, sir?"

Fletcher gazed into Dharam Singh's deep brown eyes and tried without success to plumb the depths of the photographer's mind. "That is very possible," he said, "if they find out. But is there any reason why they should? Is anyone going to tell them? Can you think of anyone who would be likely to do that?"

Dharam Singh gave the fleeting shadow of a smile. "No, Mr. Fletcher, my good sir, I can think of no one."

Fletcher smiled also. "And why would the police want the photographs anyway? If they need photographs to help them solve the crime they can surely take their own."

"Assuredly," Dharam Singh murmured. "After all, they have their own photographers."

"So now if you will let me have the prints and negatives—"

"Of course, of course."

Dharam Singh went to fetch them.

*   *   *

"You didn't tell me you took photographs," Joby said. He sounded unhappy about it. Paulina too looked worried.

"You knew I had the camera," Fletcher said. "I thought you'd know I used it."

"And you didn't tell Colonel Vincent about them?"

"No."

"Why not?" Paulina asked.

" I thought I'd like to hang on to them."

" Oh, man," Joby said; " do you like to make trouble for yourself!"

" I don't see that it's trouble."

" You will when they find out. That's like withholding information or some such. They won't be pleased about that. No, sir; not pleased at all."

" They aren't going to find out. How should they?"

" Dharam Singh—"

" He won't say anything. Will you?"

" Me!" Joby said. " You catch me goin' to the cops! You jus' catch me!"

" So it's okay. No trouble."

" You hope."

The photographs were laid out on the kitchen table. They were, as Dharam Singh had said, very good considering the conditions under which they had been taken. The bullet-holes in the heads of the five men were clearly visible, and anyone who had known them well would probably have had little difficulty in recognising them.

" See anyone there you know?" Fletcher asked.

Joby shook his head emphatically. " Not me, no. I never saw the one of them before."

The pictures of the boat had come out well also. It was possible to read the name on the bows.

" Did you ever hear of a boat called the *Halcón Español?*"

Again Joby shook his head. " It's a new one on me. Could be she come from another island or some place. You didn't see no port of origin on the stern?"

" No. Maybe it had been painted out."

" Could be."

" I have an idea Colonel Vincent had heard of it."

" What makes you think that?"

" Just a hunch. The way he reacted when I told him the name. And something he said about its not being funny. Yes, I'm pretty sure he'd heard of it."

" I don't like it," Paulina said. " I wish you'd never gone out there yesterday."

Fletcher was not at all sure that he himself would not have been happier if he had not done so. Until the previous day he had never had any contact with the police or the Leopards; now he had had contact with both, and he did not care for either lot. And he had a feeling that he was going to have more contact with them; perhaps too much. Why couldn't he have minded his own damned business and kept his nose out? Why?

Yet, looking at the matter coolly and logically, there was no reason why he should be worried. What had he done but report a crime—as any law-abiding citizen was bound to do? And though there was admittedly the question of the undisclosed photographs, that was surely of small import-ance and hardly likely to come to the notice of the police anyway. So why worry? But despite this mental argument a slight uneasiness continued to nag at him and he wished that he had had nothing to do with the business.

Joby took a newspaper called the *Jamestown Gleaner and Island Gazette*. There was nothing in it concerning the discovery of a sunken boat and five dead men, and there had been no report on the radio; so it looked as though the police were keeping it quiet.

He remarked on this fact to Joby. " Why should they do that?"

" Don't ask me," Joby said.

" You'd have thought they'd have given the press a news handout. Why would they want to keep it a secret?"

" Mebbe for the same reason they warned you not to shoot your mouth off about it. Mebbe 'cause they don't want people to know."

That was certainly the usual reason for keeping a secret, but it still provided no explanation as to why the police should not want people to know.

" There's something very fishy about this. It has a smell to it."

" You don't need to tell me," Joby said.

There was another thing : if the police intended going out to the scene of the sinking it might have been expected that they would take Joby and Fletcher along to point out the exact position where the boat was lying. But they had not done so; Colonel Vincent had made no suggestion that either Joby or Fletcher might give them any more assistance with their inquiries; he had simply said that the matter was to be left to them. It could be, of course, that they already knew precisely where the wreck of the ship was situated and could find their way to it without help from anyone else, but to Fletcher's way of thinking it would have been more natural to enlist the aid of the men who had discovered the boat. Still, if this was the way Colonel Vincent liked to work things, he had a right to use his own methods.

Joby had an engagement to take a party of elderly Americans on a trip to Mariana Bay, a holiday resort on the west coast of the island. He expected to be away until the evening. Fletcher idled away the best part of the morning, trying to convince himself that he was doing some work on the projected book, but coming up with nothing more to the point than a lot of unremarkable doodling. He

wandered out into the garden and was immediately drawn
into a game of pretend by Willie and Millie, whose impor-
tunities he always found it difficult to resist. In the afternoon
he decided to go over to Jamestown on the ferry.

The ferry was just an open boat with seats along the
sides, rather broad in the beam and equipped with a smelly
diesel engine. The passengers were mostly women going to
Jamestown to shop or visit relatives. They kept up a cease-
less chatter all the way across and dispersed on leaving the
boat like a herd of animals suddenly released from a pen.

Now that he had arrived in Jamestown Fletcher had no
particular purpose in mind. He wandered aimlessly around
the streets, feeling hot and beginning to wonder whether
the idle life was not after all somewhat over-rated. The
plain fact was—and he might as well admit it—that he was
bored. Jamestown was not like London or New York or
Paris; it did not have an infinite variety of interest; you
could very soon run out of alternative things to do to pass
the time, and all that remained then was to go and have a
drink—preferably a long and cooling one.

Fletcher was sitting at a table having his long, cooling
drink in a place that, for some reason he had never bothered
to investigate, was called Scotland House, when the two
Americans strolled over and sat down on two vacant chairs
at the same table. He was not sure they were Americans
until they started talking, but he guessed so; there was an
American look about them. And more than half the white
people you saw in Jamestown were American anyway.

One of them said: "Do you mind?" He was a lean,
desiccated sort of man with brown hair cut shorter than was
the current fashion. He looked the kind who would not give
a bent nickel for current fashion.

" No," Fletcher said; " I don't mind. Help yourselves."

The other man was not quite so lean; he had a round face and steel-rimmed glasses and he was starting to go bald. He was young enough to let it bother him and he brushed his hair carefully over the bare places, but he was not fooling anybody that way; you could see it was walking out on him and not all the hair-restorers in the world would hold it back.

" What's that you're drinking?" he asked.

" It's something they make here," Fletcher told him. " It's got some rum in it, and the juice of fresh limes and a few other things and ice, and it's very cooling. They call it a Caribbean Special."

" Sounds great," the man said. He beckoned a waiter across and ordered three Caribbean Specials. Fletcher made a slight protest, but it was waved aside. " Forget it. This one's on me. My name's Hutchins—Frank Hutchins. This is Dale Brogan."

" I'm John Fletcher."

" Pleased to meet you, John."

They insisted on shaking hands. They had strong, firm grips. Fletcher would have said they probably made quite a thing of keeping themselves physically fit.

" Are you here on holiday?"

" No," Brogan said; " I don't think you could say that. It's not a holiday; not really."

The waiter brought the drinks and Hutchins paid. Fletcher was faintly amused to see that he made a note of the amount in a small pocket-book. A careful man with money, apparently.

Brogan sipped his Caribbean Special. " Yes, very pleasant, very pleasant." He set the glass down and looked at

Fletcher. " No," he said, " we're not on holiday any more than you are."

Fletcher was startled. " What do you mean by that?"

" Well now, you're writing a book, aren't you? That's the way we heard it."

" Where did you hear it? Who told you?"

" Oh," Hutchins said, " let's not bother about who told us. Let's just say we heard. Like we heard you made a certain rather interesting discovery yesterday."

Fletcher gave the two men a closer look. " So you knew who I was? You knew before you came and sat down."

" Yes; we knew."

" You were looking for me?"

" In a way, yes."

" Why? What do you want with me?"

" We want to give you a piece of advice," Brogan said.

" More of that? I seem to be getting a lot of advice these days."

" This would be worth taking."

" What is it?"

" Forget all about what you found yesterday."

" Now that's an interesting suggestion," Fletcher said. " Do you mind telling me why I should forget it?"

" Because it would be better that way—for everybody."

" And do you think the police are going to forget it as well?"

" Never mind the police. What they do is no concern of yours."

" And if I decide not to forget it? What then?"

" That would be very foolish. You could be making a lot of unnecessary trouble for yourself."

" Maybe I could, but what's it got to do with you any-way? Who the hell are you?"

Hutchins took a long drink of the Caribbean Special and smacked his lips. " Yes, pretty good. Like you said, John, it's cooling. Now don't bother yourself with who we are. Just regard us as friends, huh? Just take it that we're looking after your best interests."

" Out of the goodness of your hearts?" Fletcher said. " That's nice; that's really nice. It's not often I get total strangers looking after my best interests. It's something for the record."

" Now don't get ruffled," Brogan said. " You may think we're interfering in something that's none of our business—"

" You're damn right, I may."

" But, believe me, it is our business. Yes indeed, very much so."

" I don't quite see that."

" Well now, you'll just have to take our word for it."

" And you're telling me to forget about it?"

" Advising you."

" In my own best interests?"

" Yes."

" In fact," Hutchins said, " we think it would be a good thing if you were to leave the island. Go back home to England."

Fletcher stared at him. " You must be joking."

" No; far from it. In fact we'd be prepared to pay all your expenses and something on top to compensate for any inconvenience. What do you say to that?"

" I say you must be very keen to get rid of me."

" Well, let's put it this way—we think that for the

moment at least your presence here could prove something of an embarrassment."

"Because I might talk about what I found?"

"That—and other considerations—yes."

"What other considerations?"

"I don't think we need go into details."

"So you don't trust me not to talk?"

Hutchins gave a faint smile. "Trust is a commodity we don't much deal in. It's not—if you'll pardon the word—to be trusted."

"And why should anything I might say—besides those other considerations—cause any embarrassment? Embarrassment for whom, for Pete's sake?"

"As I said before, I don't think we need go into that. The question is, are you prepared to accept our offer?"

"How much is the something on top?" Fletcher asked.

Hutchins glanced at Brogan, then said: "What would you say to a thousand dollars?"

"I'd say it's not enough to compensate for the inconvenience."

Hutchins frowned slightly. "How much would be enough?"

"I don't quite know. Suppose you make another offer."

"Two thousand dollars, then."

"That's better, but it's still not enough."

"We're not going any higher than that," Brogan said, and he looked annoyed.

"Please yourselves," Fletcher said. "It probably wouldn't make any difference if you did. I like it here; I'm very comfortable. You'd need to go way above the kind of price you've been offering, and even then I might not take it."

"So you're set on staying?"

" Yes."

" That's a decision you could live to regret."

" I could live to regret any decision. That's the way life is."

They didn't like it; he could see that. They had probably expected to persuade him without much trouble, but he was damned if he was going to shift just to please them. And why were they so keen on having him say nothing about the boat and the dead men anyway? What was it to them?

" You're stubborn," Brogan said. " You surely are one stubborn son-of-a-gun."

Fletcher grinned. " Well, I'm glad you didn't make it a bitch. Gun sounds much better—in that context."

Brogan did not return the grin. " It's no joke, you know. We're not playing games."

" I didn't think you were. Something maybe, but not games."

" I don't think you quite realise, John," Hutchins said, " exactly what it is you've gotten yourself into." He was adopting the reasonable, friendly tone of an older, more experienced man; a veteran talking to a rookie. " This could be dangerous."

" Are you telling me I could end up at the bottom of the sea with a hole in the head?"

" Anyone could end up that way. You'd be safer in England."

" So it's just my personal safety you're thinking about? That's why you want me to go?"

" You know damn well it isn't just that." Hutchins had abandoned the fatherly stance and his voice had hardened. " You're not that much of a fool."

" Well, thanks for the compliment."

" And it's because you're not such a fool that you should be able to see where your only interest lies. It's yourself you should be thinking about. And if you really think about yourself you'll get out, pronto."

He sat back and took a long drink of his Caribbean Special. He had had his say and was waiting for results. He set the glass down empty.

" Well?"

" Well what?" Fletcher asked.

" Are you going?"

" I don't think so."

" You sure are a stubborn son-of-a-bitch," Brogan said.

He finished his drink and they both got up and walked out. Fletcher watched their departure with some misgiving. Perhaps he was being a fool; perhaps he should have taken the money and cleared out. Certainly he was happy where he was, but it was not the only place in the world, not the only place where he could settle down and write that book —if he ever did write it. So why had he not pocketed an easy two thousand dollars and packed his bags? Well, maybe because he disliked being pushed around, being told what was best for his health and what he ought to do about it. So he would stay put; he would stay right where he was and please himself.

He drank the Caribbean Special that Hutchins had paid for and felt a touch of smug self-satisfaction at having made his own decision, at having had the strength of character to order his own affairs and never mind what other people might advise him to do. But the satisfaction failed to last long, because it occurred to him that there was not much advantage in making your own decisions if they turned out to be the wrong ones; and not much joy in ordering your own affairs, either, if the only result was to bring a load of trouble tumbling about your ears.

He ordered another drink to see what that would do for him, and it did very little. He came to the conclusion that the Caribbean Special was after all an over-rated form of refreshment and decided to go back to Port Morgan.

FIVE

POLICE

Joby arrived home earlier than expected. The Americans had soon tired of Mariana Bay and had decided to return to Jamestown. Joby had decanted them on to the pier and had taken his pay and come home.

Fletcher told him about the two men who had introduced themselves to him and made him an offer. Joby listened with a slightly worried expression on his face.

" An' you don' know who they were?" he said when Fletcher had finished. " I mean apart from the names."

" I've a good idea," Fletcher said.

" So how 'bout tellin' me?"

" Well, who else would they be but C.I.A. men? Who else would be interested enough to make an offer like that?"

" Why would the C.I.A. be that keen to get you out of the island?"

" I don't know."

" You reckon this here's a political thing?"

" It certainly begins to have that kind of look. Doesn't it seem that way to you?"

" Mebbe so," Joby said. " An' you refused the money?"

" Yes."

" Why, man, why?"

" Perhaps because I happen to like being here."

" Mebbe you shoulda taken it all the same."

" Do you mean you want to get rid of me? Is that what you're saying?"

Joby made a motion of the shoulders. " Look, you know it ain't that we don' like havin' you here. We like it fine. All the same, mebbe it'd have bin wiser to take the cash an' beat it. Seems like somethin' could be buildin' up. Like a hurricane mebbe. Best to run for shelter when there's a hurricane comin'."

Fletcher could see how uneasy Joby was, and he wondered whether it would be quite fair to him—and to Paulina and the children—if he were to stay on. If he brought trouble on himself he might bring trouble on them also. But what trouble could he bring on himself or them? It was all nonsense; no trouble was coming to him or them. Still, if Joby wanted him out of the way he would go.

" Are you asking me to leave?" he said. " Are you telling me you'd rather I wasn't here?"

Joby seemed to be avoiding his eyes, as though embarrassed by the question. " I'm leavin' it to you."

" Well," Fletcher said, " I'll think about it, if that's the way you feel. Maybe I'll go; yes, maybe I will. We'll see."

" An' take the dollars?"

" They may not still be on offer."

" Be a pity to lose all that lovely money," Joby said. " A real pity."

Fletcher was inclined to agree with him on that point.

*   *   *

He walked down to the Treasure Ship in the evening and bought himself a drink. Fat Annie served him.

" Had any more Leopards throwing their weight about?" Fletcher asked.

Annie shook her head, agitating the folds of flesh under her chin. " No, we ain't. Don't want none, neither. We had the cops, though."

" The police! What did they want?"

" Wanted to know where Mr. Dharam Singh lived."

" And I suppose you told them?"

" Why not? Ain't no secret."

" That's true," Fletcher said. " When was this?"

Annie glanced at the brass clock on the wall behind the bar. " Half an hour ago, mebbe. Somethin' wrong, Mist' Fletcher?"

" I hope not," Fletcher said. " I just hope not."

He finished the drink quickly and left Fat Annie in the Treasure Ship with a faintly puzzled expression on her broad expanse of face.

The front door of Dharam Singh's house was standing open and he could see the electric bulb shining in the glass chandelier. There was a big black car parked outside the house with nobody in it, and there were lights showing in the upper windows but there was not a peep of sound coming from up there. The sisters appeared to be keeping themselves very quiet, so perhaps they had heard the police car arrive and had decided it might be wise to attract as little attention as possible. If there were any visitors on the premises, they seemed to be keeping their heads down, too.

He did not bother to ring the bell, but walked straight in. He was damned if he knew why he did so, since the police were just about the last people he wanted to see right then; but there was a kind of compulsion driving him, an irresistible curiosity regarding what was going on. It might have nothing whatever to do with him—and he hoped it had not—but he was afraid it might, and that was the devil of it; he was only too much afraid it might.

The hall was deserted, but he knew where they were because he could hear them. He turned to the left and went down a short passageway and found himself in the doorway of the studio. The place was in a hell of a mess. There were two policemen in uniform and they had iron-tipped batons with which they appeared to be breaking everything in sight. There was another heavily-built man in plain clothes who was evidently directing operations, and Dharam Singh was there with some blood trickling from his mouth, which seemed to indicate that he had attempted to protect his property and had received a blow in the face for his pains. Mrs. Singh was there too, holding her husband's hand and watching with a horrified expression the destruction that was taking place. The rest of the family were keeping out of sight, which was probably the wisest thing to do.

When Dharam Singh saw Fletcher he tore himself away from his wife, ran to the door and grabbed Fletcher's arm.

" Mr. Fletcher, sir, tell them to stop. Tell them I am an honest, innocent man. Tell them I have done nothing wrong. Mr. Fletcher, my dear sir, I beseech you, I beg of you, save me from ruin."

" But what's going on?" Fletcher asked.

" What is going on!" Dharam Singh raised both hands above his head in a gesture of despair. " Oh, my goodness, you ask what is going on! Do you not see? They are destroying everything, everything. How can I do my work if all is gone? How can I live? How can I earn bread for my family? Mr. Fletcher, Mr. Fletcher, sir, what is to become of me?"

" There must have been some mistake."

" A mistake! Oh, my goodness, yes, a mistake!" Dharam Singh gave a hysterical laugh. " And the mistake will cost me all I possess. That is the kind of mistake it is. What am I to do? Tell me, good sir, what am I to do?"

Fletcher had no idea what to advise the photographer to do, and he still could not understand why the policemen were there; but he had no further chance of discussing the matter with Dharam Singh because the plain-clothes policeman came across to him and said:

" Are you Mr. Fletcher? Mr. John Fletcher?"

" I am," Fletcher said; and had a sudden wish that he might have been somebody else.

" My name's McIver—Sergeant McIver." The policeman flipped open a warrant card, and the name was there sure enough. " You've saved us a bit of trouble. We were coming for you."

It sounded ominous to Fletcher, and his stomach gave a kind of flutter. " For me? Why?"

" We have to take you to Jamestown. Colonel Vincent wants to see you."

" At this hour! Can't it wait until morning?"

Sergeant McIver shook his head. It was a large head, like a block of ebony topped by a narrow-brimmed straw hat. " No, sir, it cannot wait. There's a car standing outside."

" I saw it."

" You and Mr. Singh will both come with us to Jamestown." He snapped an order at the two uniformed men.

They stopped smashing things; there was little left to smash anyway.

Dharam Singh began to protest volubly. Sergeant McIver struck him on the mouth with the back of his hand, causing more blood to flow and silencing the protests.

" You didn't have to do that," Fletcher said.

McIver stared at him coldly. " Are you telling me how to do my work?"

" I'm saying it wasn't necessary to hit the man."

" Look," McIver said, " I'll decide what's necessary. You just do what you're told. Okay?"

Fletcher shrugged. It was no use arguing.

" Let's go," McIver said.

Mrs. Singh clung to her husband and started wailing, as though she saw them being parted for ever. One of the uniformed policemen tore her away from him while the other took Dharam Singh by the arm and marched him out of the room. He went quietly, dabbing at his mouth with a handkerchief, apparently resigned to his fate. Fletcher was resigned also; he went with the others out of the house and got into the car. One of the uniformed men drove, with Sergeant McIver sitting beside him. The other policeman sat in the back with Fletcher and Dharam Singh. Mrs. Singh watched them go, weeping and wringing her hands in despair.

*   *   *

Colonel Vincent looked at Fletcher in silence for a while. Captain Green was also present. It was, Fletcher reflected, a kind of reunion; but it was not one he would have wished to attend. He did not think he was very much in favour with these two men; the way Colonel Vincent was looking at him certainly indicated that he was not.

He had been separated from Dharam Singh. Singh had been led away by Sergeant McIver, a tragic expression on his face, and Fletcher had no idea what was going to happen to him. He was completely in the dark regarding the nature of Dharam Singh's crime—if there had been a crime.

At last Colonel Vincent gave a sigh. " You did not tell me everything," he said.

Fletcher tried to give the impression of a man who did not understand. " Not everything?"

" Yesterday—when you came to report the discovery of a sunken boat and five dead men. You made us believe that you had given a full and complete account of the incident; but you had not. There was one important detail that you had omitted, wasn't there?"

" I can't think of anything."

" Can't you? If that is so you must have a very short memory. But I don't believe that. I believe you are perfectly well aware of the detail I am referring to and that you purposely omitted it because you did not wish us to know about it. Mr. Fletcher, why didn't you tell us you took photographs of the boat and the men?"

" What makes you think I took photographs?" Fletcher asked; and he was wondering why Dharam Singh should have told them and why they should have rewarded him for the information by smashing up his studio and taking him into custody. It seemed a very ungrateful thing to do.

For answer Colonel Vincent unlocked a drawer in the mahogany desk and pulled out a newspaper. He opened it out and pushed it across the desk towards Fletcher.

" Take a look at that."

Fletcher took a look at it. It was not a very well printed paper but the pictures on the front page were clear enough for him to recognise them. There were three : one showing the name of the boat, *Halcón Español*; one showing a general view of the five bodies in the cabin; and another giving a close-up of one of the men and the bullet-hole in his head. There were possibly other pictures on another page, but he did not look for them; three were enough. He saw that the paper was called *Freedom*, and there was a banner headline reading : " Why is this crime being hushed up?"

Fletcher had heard of *Freedom*, though this was the first time he had seen a copy. It was an underground left-wing paper dedicated to the cause of overthrowing the President and his régime, and it was a crime even to be seen reading it. The *Freedom* press had several times been discovered and destroyed and its operators arrested, but always, after a brief interval of silence, it would spring up again like some cut-down weed the seeds of which had been left hidden in the soil.

Colonel Vincent tapped the paper with his forefinger. " In case you might imagine that this rag is already in circulation," he said, " I may as well tell you that we have here the only surviving copy. Fortunately we received information which led us to the press and we were able to seize the entire edition before distribution could start."

" That was very fortunate," Fletcher said.

" Now I ask you again : why didn't you tell us you had taken these photographs?"

" You think I took them?"

Colonel Vincent made a gesture of impatience. " Surely you are not going to be stupid enough to deny it?"

Fletcher did not answer the question. He said: "And you also think I supplied these pictures to *Freedom*?"

Vincent shook his head. "No. We know who supplied them—Dharam Singh."

Fletcher had already worked that out for himself. Singh had evidently kept copies of the photographs and as a good man of business had seen where he could sell them. Apparently he had known how to get in touch with the editor of *Freedom*, but that was not altogether surprising; he was the kind of man who would have that sort of knowledge. Only in this instance he had over-reached himself and had brought the roof down on his head. It was obvious now why the police had been smashing up his place.

"And Dharam Singh told you I took the photographs?"

Vincent smiled coldly. "There was no need. Where else would he have got them?"

"He is a photographer himself."

"But not a skin-diver."

"There are plenty of skin-divers knocking around."

"But only one who has reported finding a sunken boat."

"Some people don't like reporting things to the police."

"And some people make only incomplete reports. Come, Mr. Fletcher, tell the truth. You took the photographs, didn't you?"

There was not much point in denying it; they would not have believed him. And even if Dharam Singh had not already made a statement regarding the origin of the photographs, there could be little doubt that he soon would.

"Yes," he said; "I took them."

"And why didn't you tell us?"

"I was afraid you'd pinch the film."

Both Vincent and Green gave a laugh at that; it seemed

to touch their sense of humour. Fletcher joined in the laughter, but he was not really feeling like it. Not there; not then. His laughter was a little strained.

It all ended abruptly.

" You should have known we would need the photographs," Vincent said.

" I thought you might prefer to take your own."

It sounded thin even to him, and he could see that it sounded thin to them, too. Colonel Vincent pressed his lips together and looked sceptical.

" Why did you take the film to Dharam Singh?" Captain Green asked.

" He's the one I've always taken my films to. He's handy."

" A bit too handy."

" Did you know he was going to sell copies to this thing?" Again Colonel Vincent stabbed at the paper with his forefinger. He seemed unable to bring himself to mention the title, as though it were an obscene word.

" Of course I didn't know," Fletcher said. " I didn't even know he had kept any prints. It never occurred to me that he had."

" A man like that, you might have been sure he would. How much did you tell him?"

" In what way?"

" I mean did you tell him where you took the pictures?"

" No."

" Not that it makes any difference. The foolish thing, of course, was to let him process the film. If it was not something rather more than foolishness."

" What do you mean by that?"

" What were you intending to do with the photographs?"

" Nothing."

Colonel Vincent's eyebrows went up " Nothing! That's a little hard to believe. You take photographs and have no intention of doing anything with them?"

" Only to keep them. People do take photographs just to keep."

" But these are hardly ordinary photographs, are they? Not the sort you paste in albums or hand round to your friends. These are potentially dangerous."

" Dangerous to whom?"

Colonel Vincent leaned back in his chair and stroked his chin. " Mr. Fletcher, I find it difficult to make up my mind about you. Are you a liar or are you genuinely naïve?"

" I'm certainly not a liar," Fletcher said. " I shouldn't have described myself as naïve, either. Though of course I may be without realising it."

" Naïve or not, you are certainly fortunate."

" Am I? I don't quite see how."

" It's fortunate for you that we were able to nip this affair in the bud." Colonel Vincent took the paper between thumb and forefinger and gave it a shake, as though chastising it for the sin of existing. " If this thing had gone into circulation even a plea of naïvety would hardly have saved you from the consequences."

Fletcher experienced a sense of relief. " Then you are not going to arrest me?"

" For the present, no. But I am warning you again—don't talk about this matter. Leave it to us; it's our business, not yours."

" And what are you doing about it?"

" We are doing all that is necessary."

" Have you got a lead on the murderers?"

Vincent's expression hardened slightly. " I have already told you, Mr. Fletcher, that is not your business."

" Perhaps not, but one can't help being interested. A mystery of this kind naturally arouses the curiosity."

" Curiosity is a dangerous thing. I advise you to keep it strictly under control."

" So you don't intend to tell me anything?"

" No, Mr. Fletcher, I don't intend to tell you anything. The less you know, the better it will be for all concerned. And that includes you."

" And Mr. Singh? What happens to him?"

" Mr. Singh will have to face the music."

" He's a harmless little man."

" Perhaps not as harmless as you imagine."

" He has a wife and family. How will they manage if he isn't there to support them?"

" Mr. Singh's wife and family are no concern of mine," Vincent said.

Fletcher saw that it would be useless to plead Dharam Singh's cause; but he felt a certain degree of guilt concerning the unfortunate little man. If he had not taken the film to be processed Singh would not have been in his present trouble. On the other hand, it could not be denied that he had brought it on himself by dishonestly selling copies of the photographs to the *Freedom* newspaper. No one had compelled him to do that, least of all Fletcher. It was his own greed that was to blame for all that had happened to him and he would just have to face the consequences. Nevertheless, Fletcher's conscience was not altogether soothed by these reflections; he could not help thinking of Singh's family who were undoubtedly going to suffer. But perhaps the sisters would look after them.

" We shall, of course, require the film and any prints you may have," Colonel Vincent said. " You haven't, I hope, given any copies away?"

" No."

" Well, that at least is something to be thankful for. You don't have them on you, I suppose?"

" No; they're in my room."

" In Port Morgan?"

" Yes."

" Very well. Captain Green will go back with you and pick them up. And don't do anything foolish like trying to keep any of them. We want them all. Is that understood?"

" It's understood. And I don't want to keep any of them. I never want to see the damned things again. They've caused me enough bother already."

" You caused yourself that," Vincent said. He gave a nod to Captain Green. " All right."

" If you're ready, Mr. Fletcher," Green said, " we'll be on our way."

Fletcher stood up. Green was already moving towards the door. Vincent was stowing the copy of *Freedom* safely away.

" There is just one other thing," Fletcher said.

Vincent glanced up at him. " Yes?"

" I wonder whether you know anything of two men named Hutchins and Brogan? Americans."

Vincent's eyes narrowed slightly. " Why do you ask?"

" I had a talk with them yesterday. They advised me to leave the island."

" Did they indeed?"

" Yes. They advised it pretty strongly. They even used a bit of pressure."

" Is that so? And what was your answer?"

" I said I liked it here. It's a pleasant island."

" I hope you continue to find it pleasant."

" Is there any reason why I should not?"

Vincent did a little circular massage on his left cheek with two fingers. " That, I think, rather depends on you."

Fletcher noticed that he had not said whether or not he knew Hutchins and Brogan. It seemed fairly obvious that he had no intention of providing any enlightenment on that point, so Fletcher turned and walked towards the door where Captain Green was waiting for him. He was about to go out of the room when he heard Vincent's voice again, low-pitched and a trifle insinuating perhaps.

" Maybe you should have taken the money, Mr. Fletcher. Maybe that would have been the wisest thing to do."

Which was rather a funny thing to say, Fletcher thought, bearing in mind the fact that he had made no mention of any money.

SIX

PRESSING INVITATION

If he had had any thoughts of hanging on to a set of the photographs it would have been difficult to do so. Captain Green stayed as close to him as a Siamese twin and made a search of the room before leaving.

" Do you have a warrant to do that?" Fletcher asked.

Captain Green looked at him with a sardonic grin. " Do you have any objection?"

Fletcher doubted whether it would have made any difference if he had had any objection, and he decided to make a show of being co-operative.

" No. You go right ahead."

" Thank you," Green said; and he went right ahead, making it a very thorough search indeed. He even leafed through the copybook in which Fletcher had jotted down a few notes. " This what you write?"

" It's what I write."

" Don't amount to much, does it?"

" Not yet."

Green put the copybook down. Fletcher was glad there was nothing political in it. Green turned his attention to the camera.

" So this is what you used?"

" Yes."

" Nice job. Must have cost a lot of money."

" Too much."

It was a Japanese camera, compact but efficient. It had been secondhand when he bought it, but it had set him back quite a bit nevertheless.

Green was still holding it in his hand. " Any film in it now?"

" No," Fletcher said. He showed Green how to operate the camera. " Are you interested in cameras?"

" I'm interested in this one," Green said.

Fletcher wondered whether he was going to confiscate it, but he had had no orders from Colonel Vincent to do that and he had no sound excuse for doing so. He handed it back to Fletcher.

" Yes," he said, " a very nice job. But in future be careful what you photograph with it."

" You don't need to tell me," Fletcher said. " I don't intend photographing another boat or another dead man as long as I live."

Captain Green nodded. " That's a very wise resolution." He gave a grin. " After all, what good can it do you?"

" No good at all."

" Now," Green said, " I think I'd better have a word with Mr. Thomas."

He had his word with Joby in private. They went out into the garden and talked under the stars. When Green left, Joby came back indoors. The children were in bed, and he went into the kitchen and got himself a can of beer and brought it to the living-room where Paulina and Fletcher were waiting for him.

" You want a beer?" Joby asked, looking at Fletcher.

" I'll get it," Fletcher said. He got up. " Shall I bring you one, Paulina?"

She shook her head. " Not for me, thanks."

He got the can from the refrigerator and brought it into the living-room and sat down and drank from the can. Joby was still standing. Fletcher thought there was a sullen look about him.

" Well? What did he say to you?"

" He warned me," Joby said.

" What did he warn you about?"

" 'Bout waggin' my tongue. 'Bout the kinda places I take people to. 'Bout a lotta things. I gotta be careful or mebbe I don't have no boat no more."

" It won't come to that," Fletcher assured him. " Just be careful and keep your mouth shut and everything will be all right. And it could have been worse. Have you heard what happened to Dharam Singh?"

They had not heard. Fletcher told them.

Paulina's eyes widened and she looked scared. " They smashed up his studio and arrested him just because he processed the film for you?"

" Oh, no," Fletcher said. " If he'd done no more than that he'd have been safe enough; nobody would have laid a finger on him. But he wasn't content with that; he had to keep a set of the prints and sell them to *Freedom*."

" Oh, man!" Joby said. " That was a fool thing to do."

" Unlucky, too. The police got a tip-off and raided the press. They confiscated the entire edition before it could go into circulation, and then they paid Singh a visit and picked me up as well."

" But you're not under arrest."

" Not yet. I think you might say I'm on probation. Like

you, I've had a warning to be on good behaviour. What they'd really like is for me to leave, but they seem to be reluctant to kick me out. Maybe they think it would be bad publicity."

" And you still plan to stay on?"

" I've no other plans at present."

Joby exchanged a glance with Paulina; neither of them appeared completely at ease. Joby gave a nervous cough.

" Mebbe you should have."

" You mean you think I should leave?"

" Lotta people advisin' you to. Could be they're not all wrong."

Fletcher looked at Paulina. " Is that what you think?"

She answered with some apparent reluctance : " It's bad having the police around. They can make a lot of trouble. We don't want trouble."

" We jus' wanna live nice an' quiet, see," Joby said. " Not get mixed up in nothin'. We got kids—"

Fletcher saw that the two of them had been talking things over. Even before the arrival of Captain Green they had probably made the decision to ask him to leave. He did not blame them; they had to think about the welfare of the children as well as of themselves. They could hardly be expected to run the risk of continuing to provide lodgings for someone who had so evidently become unpopular not only with the police but with other influential people besides. That was no way to preserve a quiet life. And now the news of what had happened to Dharam Singh must have added a lot of extra weight to the argument.

" It's all right," he said. " I understand."

" It's not that we don't like having you here," Paulina said. " It's just—"

" I know."

" If we hadn' gone to look for that damn ship," Joby said, " there wouldn' have bin no trouble. All 'cause of that damn ship."

" Yes; it was a mistake. But how were we to know?"

" Well, we know now."

They finished their beer. Joby took the empty cans into the kitchen and came back.

" I'll look for somewhere else tomorrow," Fletcher said.

Joby stared at him. " You mean you still plan to stick aroun'? You still don' figure on leavin' the island?"

" No. Why should I? I'll just find other accommodation. That way you won't be embarrassed."

Joby shook his head doubtfully. " Might not be easy. Word'll get aroun'."

" You mean I could be on some kind of blacklist?"

" Don' know 'bout no list. But when people like Colonel Vincent an' Cap'n Green want you out there's ways they have of makin' things mighty hard. If you ask me, there's nobody's likely to have a room to let when you go askin'. Not even a hotel."

" So that's the way it is?"

Paulina was looking very unhappy. " We're sorry. You know we don't want to do this. We've enjoyed having you here and the children love you. But what else can we do?"

" Don't worry about it," Fletcher said. " I told you I understand. I'm not blaming you. Anything that's happened has been my own fault. I should have taken that film to the police."

" No," Joby said; " you should've destroyed it an' said nothin', not a damn thing. That was the mistake—ever goin' to them at all."

" Maybe it was. But it's done now. Tomorrow I'll look for new lodgings."

" It won't be easy," Paulina said.

*   *   *

It did not take him long to discover that she had been right. In the morning he went down to the Treasure Ship and consulted Fat Annie. If anyone knew of a room to let, she surely would. But he found Annie strangely unhelpful.

" No, Mist' Fletcher, I don't know no place you could get a room. We ain't got none here and there ain't nobody I know as has one, either."

" But there must be someone with a room to spare," Fletcher said.

" Not for you. Not for you, Mist' Fletcher."

He saw that Joby had been right : the word had got around.

" You mean there'd be a room for somebody else ?"

" Could be."

" But I've got a bad name ? Is that it ?"

" That Mist' Singh," Annie said, " he ain't come home yet, so I hear. Folks say the cops smashed his place up before they took him away. You know anything about that, Mist' Fletcher ?"

She was digging for information; he could see a kind of greed in her eye. She knew very well that he had gone to Dharam Singh's house after leaving the Treasure Ship the previous evening. Now she wanted to get the whole story from his own mouth. But he would not give her that satisfaction. He finished his drink and pushed away the empty glass.

" Well," he said, " I'm sorry you can't help me with finding a room. I shall just have to try elsewhere."

The look Annie gave him held more than a hint of mockery. " You try, Mist' Fletcher. You jest try."

He tried. He went from house to house in the burning sun and got the same answer at each one. No rooms. He was damp with sweat when he finally decided to give up the search as hopeless; he was evidently going to find no accommodation in Port Morgan.

He passed Dharam Singh's house on his way back along the main street. The front door was closed and the house seemed dead. The rust and the cracked plaster and the flaking paint looked worse than ever. He glanced up at the first floor windows and thought he caught a glimpse of one of the sisters peeping out, but he could not be sure. He was in half a mind to ring the bell and inquire whether there had been any news of the photographer, but decided that, coming from him, such an inquiry might not be welcome, and he walked on.

Joby was not at home when he got back to the bungalow. He told Paulina how unsuccessful his expedition had been. She refrained from saying that she had told him so, but it was probably in her mind.

" I'll go over to Jamestown this afternoon."

" You think you'll have any better luck there?"

" I can try."

" Well, if you think it's worth while."

She obviously did not think it was.

" I suppose you think I'm being just plain obstinate?"

" Well," she said, giving him a pretty straight look, " aren't you? Wouldn't it be more sensible to do what everyone seems to want you to do?"

" Oh, certainly it would be more sensible. But why should I? Why should I let them kick me out?"

" If they really mean to, you can't stop them."

" I know that. But I'm damned if I'll let them do it this way."

" Suppose you don't find accommodation in Jamestown. What then?"

He understood what she was saying; she meant that he could not expect to hang on to his room indefinitely while he went round hunting for new lodgings.

He smiled at her reassuringly. " Don't worry. Whether I find anything or not, I'll leave tomorrow. I won't be an embarrassment to you any longer."

He could see that she was relieved and that she was also a little ashamed of herself for being so.

" But what will you do if you haven't found a place to go?"

" Maybe I'll buy a tent and live rough."

It failed to bring a smile to her face. It was no joking matter to her.

" I'm sorry," she said. " I really am sorry."

*   *   *

He might have saved himself the bother of going over to Jamestown. When he mentioned his name rooms became suddenly unavailable: they had just been taken; they had been promised to someone else; they were being redecorated or having new floors put in or simply being taken off the market. At the hotels it was the same story, and he could only marvel at the efficiency of Colonel Vincent's organisation which had so effectively closed to him every kind of accommodation. He decided to call it a day and return to Port Morgan.

Joby had arrived home and was in the kitchen with Paulina. Fletcher gave them a brief report of his experience in Jamestown. Neither of them was surprised; they had known how it would be.

" So what now?" Joby asked.

Fletcher shrugged. " I don't have much choice. To-morrow I'll see about getting a seat on the next flight out. Or maybe I'll find a ship with a spare cabin. That's one kind of accommodation that's not likely to be barred to me."

He was feeling tired and disillusioned, and he must have sounded a trifle bitter. Both Joby and Paulina looked un-comfortable, but their discomfort was not enough to make them change their minds and tell him he could continue to occupy the room. And he would not have accepted the offer now even if they had made it. He knew they wanted him out of their hair, and the sooner the better.

" Will you try to find those Americans?" Joby asked.

" No," Fletcher said.

" You don't aim to pick up the two thousan' dollars?"

" I don't want their money," Fletcher said. Which sounded a grand renunciation but had a phoney ring to it. They all knew he had probably lost all chance of getting the dollars anyway.

He went to his room and did some packing ready for departure in the morning. He was not happy to be going, because he had liked it there; but he supposed it was the wisest course; in fact, the only one. And if he was ever going to write that book it was probably as likely to get written in a bed-sitter in London as on a West Indian island. Here the climate was too relaxing; it was too easy to be idle, just letting things drift from day to day. So okay; he would pull up stakes and go.

He hung around the bungalow until evening, but the atmosphere seemed strained. Finally he announced that he was going down to the Treasure Ship for a farewell drink, and he asked Joby whether he would like to come along.

"Not tonight," Joby said. "I got things to do."

It was a queer way of putting it: if he didn't go along with Fletcher that evening, when would he? There was not going to be another opportunity. But Joby very seldom did go to the Treasure Ship because Paulina was against it. Nevertheless, Fletcher felt a sense of grievance: Joby could surely have made an exception for his last evening.

"Well, please yourself," he said.

"Will you be late?" Paulina asked.

"I don't know. Does it matter?"

"No; it doesn't matter."

"If I get stinking drunk I'll just sleep it off on the beach or somewhere."

She looked hurt. "You know I wasn't thinking that. You never do get drunk."

It was the truth; he was only a moderate drinker. But he had felt a sudden impulse to give vent to some of the resentment he was feeling, and she had been the one to receive it. He wanted to apologise at once, or at least to make it into a joke, but he could do neither.

"There's a first time for everything," he said; and on that sour note he left them—Paulina still looking hurt and Joby with that sullen expression on his face that he had had after the talk with Captain Green.

Walking down to the Treasure Ship he felt ashamed of the way he had spoken, and he decided to make it right in the morning—or maybe that evening if he got back early enough.

The Treasure Ship was doing the usual amount of business, and it had the usual odour of spirits and tobacco smoke with a bit of human sweat mixed in to add piquancy to the brew. The light was never good in there, but this evening it was even dimmer than usual, so Fletcher concluded that there had been a voltage cut. The electricity came from the Jamestown power station and when the generators were over-loaded it was never Jamestown that took the first cut; it was Port Morgan and the other outlying places.

He walked to the bar and ordered a rum-and-ginger, and Fat Annie served it to him; but there was no big welcoming smile to go with it, and he gathered that he was no longer such a valued customer as he had once been. Annie was the kind of person who had a very exact appreciation of the way the wind lay, and if someone happened to be out of favour with the police he was also likely to be out of favour with her.

" Thought I'd call in and say good-bye," Fletcher said.

She appeared surprised. " You leavin', then?"

" In the morning."

She hardly seemed desolated by the news. " You got tired of this place, Mist' Fletcher?"

" Maybe we should say it got tired of me."

He saw that she understood. " That's the way it goes."

She moved away. He was of no further interest to her; he would be bringing no more money into the Treasure Ship.

He took his drink to a vacant table and sat down facing

the entrance. He saw a young man go to the bar and speak to Annie, and then both of them glanced in the direction of his table, so it took very little reasoning to deduce that they were talking about him. Then the young man came over and stood by the table looking down at him.

" Mr. Fletcher?"

He was the narrow-faced type of black, with a beaklike nose and slightly protruding teeth like the convex wall of a dam. He was tall and lithe, and when he moved Fletcher was put in mind of a greyhound walking; at any moment you expected him to break into an electrifying run.

" Yes," Fletcher said.

" My name's King," the young man said. " Matthew King. I'd like to buy you a drink."

" I already have a drink, Mr. King. And I don't know why you should want to buy me one."

King pulled up a chair. " Mind if I sit here?"

" The chair's free," Fletcher said.

King sat down and looked at him in silence, as though taking the size of him.

" What's on your mind?" Fletcher asked.

" I'd like to have a word with you."

" Well, go ahead. I'm listening."

King glanced over his shoulder, as though fearing that someone might be creeping up on him. He seemed nervous.

" I wonder if you could spare a little of your time, Mr. Fletcher?"

" To do what, Mr. King?"

" To meet some friends of mine."

" Why should your friends want to meet me?"

" We think you might be able to help us."

King was keeping his voice low, on what might have been described as the conspiratorial level; but nobody was listening or apparently taking any notice—except Fletcher.

"I don't know that I'm in the market to help anyone," Fletcher said. "And tomorrow I'm leaving."

Matthew King's head jerked slightly. "Leaving?"

"Yes, leaving. Never to come back."

He thought King looked perturbed. "You've made up your mind to do that?"

"Yes."

Fletcher drank some rum-and-ginger. King was drinking nothing, which was not going to make him very welcome in Fat Annie's eyes.

"Well, anyway," he said, "you could have a talk with my friends before you go."

Fletcher could not see why anyone should wish to talk to him, but he had no objection—just as long as it was friendly talk.

"Okay. You bring them along and I'll talk to them."

"Not here," King said.

"You mean I've got to go and see them?"

"They could not talk here."

"Why not?"

"Because—" King hesitated. "Well, let's say it would not be wise."

Fletcher did not care for the sound of it; there was something fishy about the thing. He had heard of people being lured into dark alleys and then being set upon and robbed, and he was not keen to become one of them; it was not the kind of experience he wanted on his last evening in Port Morgan—or at any other time for that matter.

"I'm sorry," he said, "but I'm not going anywhere. If

your pals can't come and talk with me here they'll just
have to manage without the talk."

" It's important," King said.

" Oh, I'm sure it is. So if it's that important why don't
they come to me?"

" I told you—"

King broke off abruptly and there was that slow dying
away of conversation that had occurred two evenings ago
when the men with the gold ear-rings and the fancy suits
had walked in. It was the same reason this time; they were
there again, the same two, standing just inside the room
and gazing coolly round as if searching for someone. Then
they walked to the bar with that swaggering gait they had
and spoke to Annie, and they must have been ordering
drinks because that was what came up; but once again there
was no money changing hands, and it occurred to Fletcher
that if they did all their buying on that system the cost of
living for them must have been pretty low.

And then they glanced across at his table and for a
moment he wondered whether they were looking at him or
at King; only the funny thing was that King was not there
any longer. Fletcher had not seen him go; he had been too
occupied watching the Leopards; but King had gone sure
enough and there was no sign of him anywhere in the room.
And he had not even waited to say good-bye, so maybe he
had been in a hurry.

Fletcher half-expected the Leopards to walk over to his
table and speak to him, but they were content just to look.
And then, as on the previous occasion, they finished their
drinks and swaggered out; and the tension eased and the
hum of conversation rose again as it does in a barrack room
after the orderly officer has left.

remembered that; it did nothing for his morale.

" Get in," the man said; and he sounded impatient. He prodded Fletcher with the pistol.

Fletcher looked for help, but he knew there would not be any and there wasn't. He got into the car. The man with the pistol followed him in and slammed the door. Fletcher sat wedged between the two of them. The man at the wheel started the engine and got the car rolling.

SEVEN

WITH US NOW

" Do I get told where we're going?" Fletcher asked. " Or is that a state secret?"

They both laughed. It was a deep, throaty kind of laughter and it seemed to come easy to them, though Fletcher was not sure that he cared for their sense of humour. He could imagine them laughing their heads off if somebody happened to step in front of the car and got himself run over—just as long as the car sustained no damage.

" No secret," the man who had handled the pistol said. He had put the weapon away now; he knew that Fletcher was not going to make any attempt to escape. " We're going to a place of business."

It was not the most revealing of information. A place of business could be almost anything. So could the business.

" For what purpose?"

This time they just chuckled. The chuckling was, if anything, a shade less pleasant than the laughter; there was a kind of anticipatory relish in it.

" Business," the driver said.

" What kind of business?"

" You'll see."

It was what Fletcher was all too afraid of. He decided not to ask any more questions but to sit back and await events.

Before long they were clear of Port Morgan and had got on to the road to Jamestown. It was a narrow road with a pretty rough surface, and there was not much traffic using it at that hour. This was just as well, since the man at the wheel was one of the craziest drivers Fletcher had ever come across; he seemed to have a death wish—which would have been fine if he had had only one passenger and that passenger had been the other Leopard. He could have killed the pair of them and Fletcher would not have given a damn, but he had rather more respect for his own skin and he wished he had been wearing a seat-belt because he had visions of being flung through the windscreen when the car ran off the road and hit a tree or a post or something of that description.

But nothing happened, and after about ten minutes of this hair-raising travel they were in among the shanty dwellings on the eastern fringes of Jamestown and going at a less breakneck speed. The place they finally arrived at looked like a junk-yard; it was enclosed by a corrugated-iron fence, and there were a lot of wrecked cars and worn-out refrigerators and old electric cookers and rusty oil-drums, all revealed by the headlights as they drove in through a gate which the non-driving Leopard had got down to open.

The driver stopped the car and fished a torch out of the door-pocket and switched off the lights. He got out and joined the other man, who had the pistol in his hand again. Fletcher remained in the car, not moving. The one with the pistol rapped on the door with the barrel, making a metallic, imperious sound.

" Move it, man. This here's the end of the line. From here you make with the legs."

Fletcher got out; there was no alternative. He could see the dark shape of a building of some sort in a corner of the yard. The man with the torch started walking towards it and the other two followed, Fletcher in the middle, with the pistol prodding him now and then for encouragement.

It was not a very impressive place of business; it was no more than a shack with a roof of corrugated-iron and sides of unpainted timber. The door was locked, but the man with the torch had a key; he opened it and they went in. The man with the pistol closed the door.

It seemed to be a kind of workshop; there was a bench along one side and there was a smell of oil and rubber. The man with the torch laid it down on the bench and found a hurricane lantern and lit it. He switched the torch off. The glass of the lantern was smoky and the light that came from it was scarcely brilliant, but it was enough to reveal a selection of spanners and other tools, a couple of gas-cylinders and an oxy-acetylene burner, some wooden crates, a pile of worn tyres and various odds and ends.

" So now what?" Fletcher asked. " Don't tell me you brought me here to sell me a worn tyre. I don't run a car."

They laughed again. They were in a really happy mood, and it could hardly have been the drink they had had in the Treasure Ship that was making them so cheerful; so maybe it was anticipation of enjoyment to come. The laughter stopped suddenly, as though they had both decided it was time to get down to the business.

The pistol-man said : " We got a bit of persuadin' to do."

" Persuading?" Fletcher said.

" That's right. We aim to persuade you this here island

don't have the right kind of climate for a guy like you. Bad for the health, Mr. Fletcher; real bad."

" I've never found it so."

" But mebbe this is where you begin to."

Fletcher saw that the other man had picked up a tyre lever and was hefting it in his right hand. The one with the pistol stowed it away and snatched an iron tommy-bar from the bench.

" You unnerstand, man? You get the message loud an' clear?"

Fletcher got the message very loud and very clear. Other methods apparently having failed to make him leave the island, a different kind of persuasion was about to be tried. He wondered who had given the Leopards their orders. Colonel Vincent? The C.I.A. men? President Rodgers himself? It made no difference.

They began to move towards him.

" Wait," he said. " There's no need for this. I'm leaving the island anyway. I've already decided. You don't have to persuade me."

They stopped and looked at him, but he could read no belief in their faces.

" You reckon we goin' to swaller that?" the one with the spanner said. " Man, you're crazy. You think we're that dumb?"

" It's the truth," Fletcher said. " I'm leaving tomorrow."

" You got an airline ticket?"

" No, I haven't got a ticket yet, but I'll be getting one. If I don't decide to go by sea."

" Or if you don't decide to stay on the island. Man, you ain't even tryin'. We don't buy that."

He knew that the fact was, they did not wish to buy it.

It was not simply that they had their orders to beat him up; they really wanted to do it; and whether they believed him or not, nothing was going to stop them now.

They began moving towards him again; the tommy-bar came swinging at him and he jumped aside and it missed him by an inch. He was close to the bench and he grabbed a spanner and threw it. The man who was holding the tyre lever took it in the chest, but it failed to stop him; he gave a grunt and came on like a tank. Fletcher tried to avoid the swing of the tyre lever, but it caught him on the left side just above the hip. He staggered away feeling hurt and sick, and he knew that it was not going to stop there but was going to be rough and brutal and sadistic.

Yet if they wanted him to leave the island they could not be intending to injure him too badly; they would not want to put him in hospital with broken bones or a cracked skull or a damaged kidney. But there was not much encouragement to be drawn from that reflection, because there was a hell of a lot of harm they could do without turning him into a stretcher-case; and maybe now that they had started they would not know where to draw the line; maybe they would even go the whole way, so that he ended up as an entrant not for the hospital but the mortuary stakes. That was a nice thought.

He had been getting away from them as fast as he could, but he suddenly ran out of space and found himself backed up against the pile of tyres, and they were still coming at him. He dragged the top tyre off the pile and used it as a shield, and the lever hit it and bounced off. But then the man with the tommy-bar made a jab at him through the tyre, and the end of the bar dug into his stomach and took his breath away. He began to fold and the tyre fell out of his hands; and the man with the lever took another swing at him and caught him on the right shoulder as he went down.

And then he was on the floor with the tyre under him, and there was no way of defending himself or getting away or retaliating or doing anything else except crouch there and take it.

Something hit him again in the side and he was not sure whether it was the tommy-bar or the lever, but Christ, it hurt; and he knew that if he took a blow like that on the head it could be curtains for one. But so far they had been keeping to the body, and that was bad enough.

He could hear the hissing of their breath and the scrape of their shoes on the concrete floor; and then suddenly they stopped hitting him and drew back a yard or two, and the one with the tommy-bar said:

" You gettin' the message, whitey?"

Fletcher crouched on his hands and knees, looking up at them. The lantern was behind them and their faces were shadowed, but he could see the gold ear-rings swaying and glittering, and he really hated them then; hated them so much that he knew that if he had had a gun in his hands he would have shot them both without compunction. But he had no gun, no weapon of any kind, and he could only look at them and wait, knowing that it was not finished yet, that this was only a breather and that soon they would start again with their iron bludgeons, hammering away at his body and loving it, loving it, damn them.

" You bastards!" he said. " You bloody bastards!"

That seemed to amuse them, too; the laughter came spilling out of their broad mouths while the ear-rings danced a jig.

"You feelin' sore, man? You got bruises mebbe?" the one with the tyre lever said. "You ain't seen nothin' yet. Why, man, you stick aroun' on this here island an' I promise you get sumpin' worse'n that. If I was you I'd get out just as quick's I can."

"I am getting out. I told you."

"Sure, man, sure. We heard. But jus' so's you don' go forgettin' what you gotta do, reckon we better give you a bit more of the memory treatment. What you say, man?"

"Keep away from me."

They laughed again and started moving towards him, swinging the iron clubs. But they were still a yard away from him when the door opened and Mr. Matthew King stepped into the hut.

King had a machete in his hand and the broad curving blade looked as though it had had a recent visit to the grindstone; the edge had the bright cold gleam of razor-sharp steel. King moved further into the hut and another man came in behind him. The other man also had a machete in his hand, and he was as tall as King and twice as wide; he looked as though he could have pushed his way through the wall of the hut if the door had not been open.

"Ha!" King said; and Fletcher could see no sign of nervousness in him now. A little anger perhaps, but that was all.

The Leopards swung round to face the door and for a moment seemed taken out of their stride. For a moment they hesitated; then, as though with a common impulse, they dropped the lever and the tommy-bar and went for their guns. But it was too late; King and the other man stepped briskly forward and the machetes gleamed in the lantern light. There was a vicious swishing sound and then there was blood spurting and two men sinking to the floor and dying. So quickly had it been done, and with such expert precision, that it was hard to believe it had really happened. But the bodies were there and the blood was spilling out on to the floor, and that was proof enough that it had been no illusion.

" Get their guns," King said in a low, utterly unemotional voice. " Quickly."

The other newcomer dropped his bloodstained machete, stooped and took the pistols from the dead men. Fletcher was struggling to his feet. King dropped his machete also and helped him up.

" Are you hurt?"

" They hit me a few times," Fletcher said.

" Any bones broken?"

" I don't think so."

" You should have come with me," King said.

Fletcher looked at the dead men and felt his stomach turn. " Would I have had better treatment?"

King smiled grimly. " You think this might have happened to you?"

" The possibility did cross my mind."

King shook his head. " We don't plan to kill you, Mr. Fletcher. We want you alive. We want you very much alive. Yes, sir."

The big man had stuck the pistols in his belt. " Let's go," he said. " Let's go." He had a deep, rumbling voice, like an echo in a vault.

" Okay, Lawrence," King said. " Come along, Mr. Fletcher; it's time we were away from here. You're with us now."

Fletcher decided not to disagree; he felt in no condition

for argument. They walked to the door. Lawrence picked up the hurricane lantern and followed them. When King and Fletcher were out of the hut he turned and flung the lantern at one of the wooden crates. The glass shattered and the oil spilled out and took fire immediately.

" Hurry now," King said. " No time to waste."

When they reached the gate the flames were visible through the window of the hut. There was a big blue Ford parked outside the yard with someone in a floppy sun-hat sitting at the wheel. King opened the nearside rear door.

" Get in, Mr. Fletcher."

Fletcher's hesitation was only momentary. With the blaze getting a real hold on the hut, it was not a healthy area to hang around in, and he had never felt less like taking a brisk walk or a hard run than he did just then. He got in and King followed him. The big man got in beside the driver. Half a second later they were away.

No one said anything until they were clear of Jamestown and heading north, away from the coast. It was one of the quietest car rides Fletcher could remember. Finally he said :

" So you're kidnapping me ?"

" I'd have called it rescuing," King said. " You weren't doing too well when we arrived."

Fletcher acknowledged the truth of that. " I suppose you followed us from Port Morgan ?"

" That's so. But we lost touch for a time. We had to hunt around to find the place. That's why we were late."

" You knew where they would go ?"

" We had a good idea."

" Was it necessary to kill them ?"

" Well, what do you think ? They would have used the guns. We had to be quick. It was either kill or be killed."

Fletcher could appreciate the logic in that. And had he not himself felt a desire to kill the men? So who was he to criticise? It had been brutal nevertheless.

" And now where are you taking me?"

" Maybe you'd better ask the driver," King said.

The driver turned and looked at Fletcher for a moment. " We're going home."

It was the first time he had caught a glimpse of the driver's face; the floppy hat had effectively screened it from his view. Therefore he had not realised that the driver was female and white. The accent said she was American, too.

" I should have introduced you," King said; and he sounded faintly amused. " Leonora, this is Mr. John Fletcher."

" I guessed," she said. " Who else could it be? Hi, John."

" Hi, Leonora," Fletcher said. " Where's home?"

" Didn't anyone ever tell you? Home is where you make it."

" Thanks," he said. " Now I know everything."

He began to wonder how an American girl came to be mixed up with people like King and Lawrence, people who could do such deadly work with machetes; but it was not a question to go into just then. Besides, he did not yet know who the two men were, or why they should be so interested in him. But perhaps all would eventually be made clear. One thing at least began to look more and more certain as the Ford got further and further away from Jamestown: he was not likely to be back at Joby's very early. In fact, it seemed more than possible that he would not return that night. Which was likely to throw his plans for a morning departure sadly out of gear.

" Do we have far to go?" he asked.

" It's not that big an island," King said. " How could it be far?"

*   *   *

It was a large rambling old house somewhere in the hill country on the northern side of the island. To get to it they had to leave the tarred highway and take to some roads that were even worse than the one between Jamestown and Port Morgan; really rough, with some pretty steep gradients and hairpin bends that called for no little skill on the part of the driver. Picked out by the headlights of the Ford, some of the going looked hazardous indeed, and Fletcher decided that he himself would have preferred to make the drive in daylight.

He was relieved when they reached the end of the journey and Leonora brought the car to a halt in front of the house. There seemed to be no lack of lights around the place, and he concluded that a generator was working somewhere, since it was in far too isolated a situation to gets its electricity in any other way. They got out of the car and climbed some wide stone steps to a spacious terrace of the same material. From the terrace they went into the house, which at first glance seemed to be an expanse of polished wood floors and heavy furniture that could well have been there from the time when the building had been completed.

The man who greeted them appeared to be about fifty; his hair was greying and his skin was tan rather than black. He was of medium height, lean and rather handsome, elegantly dressed, and with a keenly intelligent look about him. Fletcher had the feeling that he had seen him somewhere before, but he could not remember where or when.

" Well, Mr. Fletcher," the man said, " I'm very glad you were able to come."

" I didn't have much choice," Fletcher said.

" No? You will have to tell me about that. However, the main thing is that you are here." He held out his hand and it would have seemed ridiculous as well as rude to refuse it. The grip was firm but not prolonged. " My name is Conrad Denning."

Fletcher knew then why he had had that impression of having seen the man before. Different though the two might be in physique and many other ways, there was nevertheless a certain unmistakable facial resemblance between Mr. Denning and President Clayton Rodgers. And this was really not so very surprising, since Denning and Rodgers happened to be cousins.

" Mr. Fletcher," Denning said, " you are welcome to my house, very welcome indeed."

EIGHT

SO MANY ENEMIES

They talked in a large comfortable drawing-room which opened on to the terrace, and Fletcher kept remembering things he had heard about Conrad Denning. Like his cousin, Denning had studied law in the United States, and he had a practice in Jamestown. He was reputed to be a wealthy man and had at one time been prominent on the political scene, but he had opposed Clayton Rodgers and had lost; as Rodgers's star ascended, so Denning's faded—at least in the political sense. It was said that he had only avoided imprisonment or banishment from the island by agreeing to abandon politics altogether and never again meddle in affairs of state. So he had retired into the background and had concentrated on his legal business. It was safer than fighting the President.

"You are no doubt wondering," Denning said, "what there can possibly be that we should wish to talk to you about."

Fletcher smiled. "I'd have to be pretty incurious not to wonder about that. You went to some lengths to get me here."

"It became a little more complicated than we had anticipated. We were not expecting you to be carried off by those thugs. Incidentally, what did they want of you?"

"They wanted to convince me that the island climate was bad for my health and that I ought to leave without delay."

"But I believe you had already decided to do that. Didn't you tell them so?"

"I told them, but I don't think they believed me. Either that or they wanted to make sure I didn't change my mind. And I think they took pleasure in the job for its own sake; they seemed to get quite a kick out of it."

"They would. How are you feeling now?"

"Stiff and sore."

"It could have been worse. If help had not arrived—"

"I'm not disagreeing with that," Fletcher said. "But you still haven't told me the reason. Why did you want to bring me here? What do you want to talk about?"

"About a sunken boat and five dead men, shall we say?"

Fletcher was not surprised. It seemed to be what everyone wanted to talk to him about. "Yes," he said; "it had to be that. But how did you hear about it?"

"Information has a way of getting around once it's been set moving. And the name of the boat was, I believe, *Halcón Español*. Right?"

Fletcher remembered the warnings he had had. "I don't know that I want to talk about it."

"Because the police told you not to? Because Colonel Vincent advised you to keep a still tongue, perhaps?"

Fletcher reflected that Denning seemed to know a great deal. Information certainly had a way of getting around, though he could not understand how.

"There were others."

" Ah, yes. Americans, possibly?"

So he knew that too. Or guessed.

It was the girl who broke in now. She was sitting on a sofa with her legs tucked under her and her shoes kicked off; and now that he could see her clearly Fletcher had to admit to himself that she had a lot going for her physically. He would have put her age at about twenty-five or so, and she was dark-haired, sloe-eyed, and with a pretty good sun-tan, which was not surprising considering the climate. She was wearing a shirt and slacks, and he thought she looked fine in them. She would have looked fine in just about anything—or nothing, if it came to that.

" Look, John," she said, using his first name in that easy way Americans had, " why bother about all that official secret garbage? We know you found the boat, so let's take it as read, shall we?"

" Well, if you know all about it already," Fletcher said, " why did you go to the trouble of bringing me here? You could have saved yourselves a deal of bother."

She glanced at Denning, leaving it to him.

Denning said: " There's something else we want to know. What happened to the other photographs?"

" What do you mean by other photographs?" Fletcher asked.

" I mean there was one set of prints that Dharam Singh held back and then sold to *Freedom*. They were destroyed when the press was raided by the police. Singh may have kept others, but they will also have been destroyed or confiscated by the same people. That leaves the negatives and the prints he made for you. What we should like to know is, do you still have them?"

Fletcher shook his head. " No."

Denning seemed disappointed. " No?"

" You appear to be so very well informed," Fletcher said, " I should have thought you would have known that when the police picked up Dharam Singh they picked me up too. They guessed that I must have taken the photographs and they weren't at all pleased with me for not having mentioned them when I reported finding the boat. I think it was touch and go whether or not they slung me in the jug, but finally I was let off with a caution. Then a Captain Green accompanied me back to Port Morgan and picked up the prints and negatives. He seemed to be in half a mind to take the camera as well, but he let me keep it. I suppose he thought I was hardly likely to go out to the wreck again and take another set of photographs."

" And you didn't keep any copies?"

" How could I? He was breathing down my neck all the time like a damned bloodhound."

" I thought you might perhaps already have hidden some away."

" Why the devil should I do that?"

Denning sighed. " Why, indeed! I suppose it never occurred to you that there might be such a demand for them?"

" You can bet your life it didn't. And I still don't understand why there's such a song and dance about them."

He thought Denning might give him an explanation, but he was to be disappointed in that. Denning was silent; he seemed to be thinking.

Fletcher looked at King. " You seem to have had all your bother for nothing. No pictures."

" You should be glad we took the bother," King said.

" Oh, I am. Believe me, I'm very grateful."

Denning gave him a speculative look. " Do you really mean that?"

" Of course I mean it. Do you think I enjoy being beaten up?"

" In that case perhaps you would be prepared to show your gratitude in a practical way."

Warning bells started ringing in Fletcher's head; he had a nasty feeling that he was about to be asked to do something which might get him into more trouble. And he wanted no more; he just wanted to get away from it all; far, far away.

He answered warily: " What kind of way would that be?"

" You said just now you supposed Captain Green must have thought it was hardly likely you'd be fool enough to go back to the wreck and take some more pictures."

" Now wait," Fletcher said. " Don't tell me you're going to ask me to do just that."

They were all staring at him now; he could almost feel them putting the pressure on him with their eyes.

" Why not?" Denning said.

" Why not! I'll tell you why not. Because it's crazy, that's why not; just downright crazy."

" Why crazy?"

" Well, for one thing because there wouldn't be a chance of doing it. There'll be police hanging around. They'll be dredging up the bodies. Maybe salvaging the boat."

" I don't think so," Denning said. " I don't think the police will take any action of that kind whatever."

" You may not think so, but that's hardly good enough, is it? And even if they aren't there, it wouldn't be the same, you know."

" In what way?"

" The corpses. I don't know a lot about such things, but I'd say they'll be deteriorating all the time. The pictures might not be so good."

" That's a risk we'd have to take."

Which was all very fine for him, Fletcher thought. Who did he imagine was the joker who would be taking the risk?

" It can't be done anyway."

" No?" Denning said. " Why not?"

" I haven't got my camera and diving gear."

" But you know where they are."

" And you think I can simply walk in and pick them up and tell Joby Thomas I want him to take me out to the same place? He'd never do it; never in a million years."

" I was not suggesting that you should go with Mr. Thomas. This time we will provide the boat."

" You?"

" Certainly. That's no problem."

" But there's still the other problem."

" You mean getting the camera?"

" Yes."

" But it could be done. And you don't need to bother about the diving gear; we can provide that too."

" Are you suggesting I go back tonight and pick up the camera?"

" No; it is too late and there would be the risk of the car being stopped. I have a feeling, Mr. Fletcher, that after what has happened you may be on the police wanted list. Don't you think it's possible?"

" That's all I needed," Fletcher said. " So how do you

expect me to get the camera? Do I just go back to Port Morgan tomorrow in broad daylight?"

Denning shook his head. " No; that would be very unwise indeed."

" So what do you suggest?"

" That you wait until tomorrow night."

" And then go and pick it up?"

" Yes."

" I'm sorry," Fletcher said, " but it's not on; it's simply not on."

Denning frowned. " You mean you don't think you can get the camera?"

" Well, it could be a bit dodgy; but I wasn't thinking about that part of the operation. It's the other part that really gives me the willies."

" You mean the underwater work?"

" Yes."

Surely you are not telling me you're afraid?" Denning sounded incredulous.

" That's exactly what I am telling you, and I don't mind admitting it. But even if I wasn't, I'm not sure I'd want to do it."

" So much for gratitude," Leonora said.

There was enough scorn in her voice to sting a little, and Fletcher turned on her sharply.

" Don't push it too hard. I don't think anyone was acting solely in my interests. Anyway, I've had strict orders not to meddle any further in this business."

" Orders from the police?"

" Yes."

" You think you owe them anything? Looks to me like they're not using any kid-glove methods with you."

" You mean the beating up? That wasn't the police; it was another lot."

" We know who it was; but all orders come from the same source, ultimately. They're all working for the same man. You know that. Are you going to take this sort of thing lying down? Don't you want to hit back at them? Don't you have any spirit, for Pete's sake, or are you just one big spineless slob?"

He was stung again by her words and the tone in which they were spoken, though he knew that that was her purpose. She wanted to goad him into doing what they asked. But he saw no reason why he should, and a lot of very good reasons why he should not.

" If you're so keen on the damned photos," he said, " why don't you get somebody else to take them? Why doesn't one of you go down there and have a shot at it?"

" We don't have anyone with the necessary experience, that's why. If we had, do you think we'd bother with you?"

Fletcher laughed. " So now we're getting to the truth. You really need me, don't you?"

" You need us, too," Denning said softly.

Fletcher glanced at him quickly. " How do you figure that out?"

" You're in our hands. We could hand you over to the police."

" The police haven't got anything on me."

" No? You think they won't connect the death of two men in a burnt-out hut in a junk-yard with you? There'll be witnesses to swear that you left Port Morgan with the two men in a car. They'll take fingerprints from the car and match them up with yours. Would you like to make a bet you didn't touch anything? Think about it, Mr. Fletcher; think about it."

Fletcher thought about it and saw the kind of situation he was in. If the police got hold of him again they would surely lock him away this time, and maybe he would never get out again alive, however hard he tried to explain things and however much he might protest his innocence. Protestations would not be enough, not nearly enough.

" With us," Denning said, " you are safe. Being with us is possibly the only way you are safe. You have so many enemies, so few friends. Think about it."

It was a situation that left him little choice. He was in it now, in it up to the neck, and he could see no way out.

" I came to write a book," he said, " and look what's happened."

" You'll still live to write the book," Denning said. " But you're with us now."

It was what King had said. Fletcher was beginning to think it might be true.

" So I'm to stay here tonight?"

" There is a room prepared for you?" Denning said.

*   *   *

It was a large pleasant room with a balcony. From the balcony there was a magnificent view, as he discovered when he got up in the morning. From the terrace in front of the house the ground fell away fairly steeply at first, then more gently. He could see the road up which they had come the previous night; it was like a narrow stream meandering between outcrops of rock, trees, undergrowth; creeping ever downwards until it finally disappeared from sight. To the left and right the hills were green with the abundant vegetation, mist still rising like steam from hollows into which the sun's heat had not yet penetrated. It was the kind of country in which a man could vanish and evade pursuit, perhaps for years, perhaps for ever. Guerrilla country.

He went to the bathroom and found that a razor had been provided. He shaved and took a shower and went down to breakfast. Leonora was there, but not the others. She was wearing a multi-coloured shirt and a brief denim skirt. It was the first glimpse he had had of her legs and he could find nothing wrong with them. Taken all in all, he decided that she was the kind of girl it would be pleasant to have breakfast with; and perhaps not just once, either.

She cocked her head on one side and gave him a critical inspection. " Um!" she said. " You look well enough. How do you feel?"

" A lot better than might have been expected," Fletcher told her. " Apart from a few bruises and some stiffness here and there, I feel fine."

" That's good. We wouldn't have wanted a cripple on our hands."

" You're looking at it simply from your own point of view, of course?"

She lifted an eyebrow. " Oh, come now, John; you're not expecting tea and sympathy and all that jazz, are you? This is a tough, cynical old world, and you have to face up to it."

" What you're telling me is that you and the others rescued me solely for your own advantage and that you don't give a damn whether I'm alive or dead, except in so far as it affects your plans, whatever they may be. Is that it?"

She smiled. " I believe you're feeling hurt. You really are looking for sympathy."

" I'm not hurt," Fletcher said; " except physically. But I resent being used. By anybody."

" We all use other people; it's a fact of life. You're using us."

He supposed it was true in a way, though it was hardly the same thing; he had not forced himself on them. But he decided not to get into an argument about it; and at that moment King and Lawrence appeared, followed a little later by Conrad Denning.

Breakfast was served on the terrace by an elderly black manservant, and there was that magnificent view which Fletcher had seen from his balcony.

" You have a fine place here," he said.

Denning agreed. " I am lucky. Perhaps I should feel guilty about having so much."

" And do you?"

" A little. Sometimes I ask myself why one man should have so much more than another."

" It's always been like that. Always will be."

" Is that what you think?"

" I'm not expecting to see any big change in my lifetime. Even in communist countries there's inequality."

" Well, we shall see," Denning said; " we shall see."

He left soon after breakfast on his way to Jamestown, explaining that he had legal business to attend to; which served to remind Fletcher that this cousin of President Rodgers was still a practising lawyer. He drove away in an open Aston Martin, another example of his somewhat opulent style of living; and Fletcher could not help wondering how such a man came to be involved with people like

King and Lawrence, or even Leonora. And if it came to that, what was Leonora doing there anyway?

King and Lawrence soon disappeared, perhaps by previous agreement, and he was left with the girl for company. He suspected that she had been deputed to keep him under surveillance; which was just fine as far as he was concerned; he could think of no one he would rather have had to keep him under surveillance. She took him on a tour of the property; there was an extensive garden on several levels with a stream running through it; there were waterfalls and shade trees and rocky pools and rampant vines and creepers; and there was not another building in sight. They sat by one of the pools and watched the water cascading into it from a lip of rock above.

" What are you doing here?" Fletcher asked. He had already discovered that her surname was Dubois, which suggested French ancestry.

" I'm a journalist," she said.

" A journalist!" If she had said a hairdresser it would hardly have seemed less likely.

" Well, don't look so surprised. Is there anything strange in that?"

" Not in itself perhaps. It's the situation that makes it surprising. Are you telling me that you're practising journalism right here and now?"

She smiled enigmatically. " You might say that."

" I don't understand. What goes on here? What is everyone up to?"

" You would like to know?"

" Of course I'd like to know. When I'm involved in something as deeply as I'm involved in this, I naturally feel an interest in what it's all about. Wouldn't you?"

" Yes," she admitted, " I suppose I would."

" Well, are you going to tell me?"

She shook her head. " I'm afraid not. Not yet."

" It's political, isn't it? Mr. Denning is not supposed to touch politics, but I'll bet he is. He's got his fingers in something, and if President Rodgers found out about it he'd be in real trouble, wouldn't he?"

" You're just speculating," she said.

" I know I'm speculating, but it's pretty accurate speculation, isn't it? What I still can't figure out is where you fit in."

She smiled again. " Well, you work on it, John. Just go on working on it, and maybe you'll finally come up with an answer."

With those legs and that figure and those lovely dark eyes and that enigmatic smile playing around her lips, she was really something. You could travel a long way and never come across anyone half as attractive as Leonora Dubois, and he toyed with the idea of telling her so, but decided not to. Let it wait awhile.

" Oh," he said, " I'll work on it. There's nothing I can think of I'd rather work on."

*   *   *

Denning returned late in the afternoon. King and Lawrence also turned up. Fletcher wondered where they had been, but he did not ask; he doubted whether they would have told him if he had. Denning called a conference to discuss plans for the picking up of the camera.

" Can you get into the house without rousing the family?" he asked.

" I've still got a key," Fletcher said. He had had one for quite a while, so that he could come and go as he pleased. " But there's no need to creep in like a thief. I'm not going to steal anything."

" All the same," Denning said, " I think it would be better if Mr. Thomas didn't see you."

Fletcher had a feeling that Denning had picked up some information in Jamestown which he was not revealing; but again he asked no questions.

" I suggest you get there at about one o'clock in the morning," Denning said. " Will they be asleep by then?"

" Unless they've changed their habits."

Denning took a piece of notepaper from a small writing-desk and drew a sketch-map of the Port Morgan peninsula.

" Whereabouts is the house?"

Fletcher marked the approximate position and Denning nodded.

" Good. Then you can approach it from the beach on the seaward side? Is that so?"

" Yes; but the road is on the other side."

" You will not be going by road," Denning said. " You will be going by sea."

NINE

NIGHT OPERATION

They picked up the boat at a little place on the north coast where an inlet from the sea formed a natural harbour. It was a trifle over half an hour's journey in the Ford and it had been dark before they started. Leonora again did the driving and she was again dressed in shirt and slacks, but this time she had left the hat behind. King and Lawrence also came along. Fletcher was not sure whether they were armed, but he suspected they might be. He just hoped there would be no call for violence; there had been enough of that the previous evening.

The boat was in amongst a lot of other boats and they had to get to it along a crazy sort of board-walk after parking the car. There were a few lights hanging on posts, but the illumination was not very brilliant and there was little sign of activity around the boats. Fletcher had a guilty feeling and was keeping an eye open for any policemen who might be prowling about, but he could see none, and the girl and the other men seemed completely unworried.

It was not a large boat, but it looked fast. Perhaps Denning enjoyed a bit of water-skiing when he felt like relaxing, or maybe he just liked a speedy boat the way he liked a fast car. It was secured by a rope at the bows to a post on the board-walk, and there was a cabin not much bigger than a fair-sized dog-kennel and a glass windscreen to catch the spray. They went on board and Lawrence got the engine started while King cast off, and a few minutes later they were clear of the harbour and heading towards the eastern curve of the shore.

It was a fine clear night with all the stars shining as brightly as newly-minted coins, and Fletcher might have enjoyed the trip if he had not been worrying about possible snags ahead. Suppose the police were watching Joby's bungalow, waiting for him to return. It was not unlikely; in fact, when he came to think about it, it seemed the most probable thing in the world and he wondered why it had not occurred to any of them when they were planning the operation.

He suddenly felt Leonora's hand on his arm. He turned his head and could make out the pale oval of her face under the dark hair.

" What are you thinking about?" she asked.

He told her.

" You worry too much," she said.

" Don't you think there's any cause for worry?"

" It doesn't help."

" I know it doesn't help, but nobody ever stopped worrying because of that."

" Everything will be all right. You'll see."

" I hope so," he said. " I just hope so." But he doubted it. More likely that everything would be all wrong. He listened to the powerful note of the engine and the swish of water streaming back from the bows, and all the time there was a sick flutter in his stomach and he wished he had been a thousand miles away and had never heard of a boat called

Halcón Español. It would have been better if that Spanish Hawk had never flown into his life.

Just over an hour later they turned the headland and were running south along the eastern coast about half a mile out from land. Before long the shoreline curved sharply away to the westward, but Lawrence kept the boat's head still pointing due south, cutting across the wide bay on the southern side of which was the Port Morgan peninsula.

Lawrence had not been pushing it, but the boat had been going along at a useful rate and the engine had never faltered. Nevertheless, it was getting on for one o'clock when they reached the place where they had planned to go ashore. Lawrence reduced the speed and the engine note dropped to a low mumble, and he made a turn to starboard and ran on under the stars with no light showing. There was a glimmer of white beach ahead with a dark line of palm-trees beyond it, and they came in gently and slid the keel into the sand. Lawrence stopped the engine and King said :

" You know the way from here?"

" I know the way," Fletcher said.

" I'll come with you."

" There's no need for that," Fletcher said quickly. He was not keen to have King with him; this was something he preferred to handle on his own. That way there would be no shooting.

But King just said again : " I'll come with you."

It was no time to argue. Fletcher clambered up to the bows and jumped down into the shallow water. King followed him as he made his way up the beach, and when he turned he saw that Leonora had come with them.

" Look," he said, " do we need a crowd?"

" You may need some help," she said.

" If I need help it's going to be a shambles."

" All right, so it's going to be a shambles. Get moving."

He gave a sigh of resignation and got moving. The other two followed. Lawrence stayed with the boat.

They came to the palm-trees and went in among them. It was darker there. Fletcher had a torch in his pocket, but he had no need to use it; he knew the way well enough, for he had often used this route from Joby's to the beach. The three of them kept close together and in a little while they were clear of the palms. There was rough grass underfoot and the ground rose slightly to a low ridge before descending again on the other side. The shadowy outline of Joby's bungalow came in sight soon after that, with the trees in the back garden, and a few yards further on they came to the fence.

They all halted. The bungalow was dark and silent. There was no sound but the dry rustle of leaves and the soft murmur of the sea.

" You'd better wait here," Fletcher said.

He felt the brief touch of Leonora's hand. " You won't be long?"

" I won't be long," he said; and hoped it was the truth. If he were long it would mean that he had hit trouble.

He climbed over the fence and made his way past the hammock slung between the two coconut palms and round to the front of the bungalow. He took the key from his pocket and groped for the keyhole. He inserted the key very carefully and turned it with equal care. There was a faint click as the tongue of the lock slid back. He turned the knob gently and pushed the door open.

There was a mat which the bottom of the door just

touched with a light brushing sound that seemed abnormally loud to his ears. The hall was no more than a narrow passageway and his room was on the right. He left the front door standing half-open and moved in the darkness to the door of his own room, opening it with the same infinite care he had used with the other. He stopped just inside the room and took the torch from his pocket and switched it on.

In this small light the room appeared to be exactly as he had left it : the suitcase he had packed was on the floor half under the bed and there was a canvas holdall with a zip-fastener lying on top of the wardrobe. He laid the torch on the bed and picked up the suitcase and put it on the bed also. He took down the holdall and filled it hurriedly with the things he had not already packed; then zipped it up.

He had put the camera on the dressing-table after Captain Green had had his look at it, and now he went to pick it up—and that was the first shock. It was no longer there.

He stood perfectly still for a few moments, beginning to sweat and wondering who the devil could have taken it, until suddenly he remembered that before leaving to go down to the Treasure Ship he had put it away in the bottom drawer of the dressing-table. He bent down and pulled out the drawer, and it was one of the tight-fitting kind that nobody has yet succeeded in pulling out silently. It seemed to make a hell of a noise and nearly dragged the dressing-table with it, and by the time he had got it open he was really sweating. But the camera was there, and the films and all the rest of the gear, and he stowed the lot in a big leather case and slung the carrying-strap over his shoulder.

He picked up the holdall and suitcase with one hand and switched off the torch and dropped it into his pocket—and that was when he had the second shock. There was a sharp click and the light came on in the room and there was Joby Thomas standing in the doorway with a machete in his hand.

"So you came back," Joby said softly. He was naked except for a pair of cotton trunks, and his skin gleamed like polished ebony.

"Yes," Fletcher said, "I came back."

"Why?"

"To get my things."

"You shoulda come in daylight, not like a thief in the night."

"There were reasons."

"Sure, reasons. I bet. Now what you aimin' to do?"

"I'm clearing out, Joby. Like I promised."

"No," Joby said.

Fletcher looked at him. There was something strange about Joby; he was not the old friendly companion he had once been; he had altered, hardened; there was even a kind of shiftiness in his eyes, a reluctance to meet Fletcher's gaze. Above all, there was the machete in his hand. Fletcher experienced a feeling of uneasiness that he had never previously known in Joby's company.

"What do you mean—no?"

"I mean you ain't clearin' out. Not now."

"You're stopping me?"

"That's right," Joby said. "I'm stoppin' you."

"Why, Joby, why?"

"'Cause you're wanted; that's why."

"Wanted?"

" For murder."

" Now look, Joby," Fletcher said, " you don't really believe I killed anyone."

" I don't know what you done. All I know's the cops want you for murder an' I gotta hold you."

Fletcher could see how it was : Joby was protecting himself. Perhaps he had been warned that if his lodger came back he was not to let him go until the police came to pick him up. Joby might not like doing it; he certainly did not look happy; but he had to protect his own interests, and he had his family to think about. The family would certainly weigh more heavily with him than any past friendship with Fletcher.

The suitcase and holdall were beginning to put a strain on his left arm, and he set them down. Joby filled the doorway and there was no possibility of brushing past him.

" Would you use the machete?"

" You better not make me," Joby said.

" You're going to stand there and keep guard on me till morning?"

There was a hint of uncertainty in Joby's eyes. He had probably not thought things out to the conclusion. It was a situation that could soon have become tedious if there had not been another interruption.

" Drop the machete or I'll shoot you in the back," Leonora said.

Fletcher could just see a part of her behind Joby; the rest was hidden. She must have become worried at the amount of time he was taking to fetch the camera and have decided to investigate, leaving King to keep watch. She had come in very silently by way of the open front door, so that neither he nor Joby had heard her; they had both been unaware of her presence until she had spoken.

Joby had stiffened but had not moved. The machete was still in his hand, dangling at his side. He had been taken completely by surprise and seemed at a loss what to do. The girl helped him to make up his mind by pressing the muzzle of the pistol she was holding into the small of his back. It must have felt cold on his bare skin, and Fletcher saw him give an involuntary shiver, though it might not have been entirely because of the cold.

" Drop it," she said.

Joby dropped it and it fell with a slight clatter to the floor.

" Now go into the room," Leonora said.

Joby walked into the bedroom and she followed him in and told him to turn round. He did so. She spoke to Fletcher.

" Are you ready?"

" I'm ready," Fletcher said.

It was her turn to show a little uncertainty. " We ought to go; but what do we do with him?"

Fletcher looked at Joby. " I don't think he'll make any more trouble. What do you say, Joby?"

Joby gave a resigned shrug of the shoulders. " What more you reckon I can do? I done what I had to, an' it didn' work. Ain't nothin' more to do now."

" Right, then," Leonora said. " Let's go, John."

She picked up the machete and carried it out, just to make sure Joby got no bright ideas about making use of it again. Fletcher picked up his luggage.

" I'm sorry, Joby."

" Sure, sure," Joby said. " It's the way it goes, man."

Fletcher heard Leonora calling him. She sounded impatient.

" I've got to go."

" Sure," Joby said.

He went out of the room and caught a glimpse of Paulina in a nightdress, looking scared.

" Good-bye, Paulina," he said. " I'm sorry it had to end this way."

He really was sorry about it, and he hoped they would not be persecuted because of him. But there was nothing he could do about it, except maybe stay there and wait for the police to pick him up on a murder rap; and that was too much of a sacrifice to expect of any man.

Leonora was waiting for him outside. They went round to the back garden and she threw the machete away. Fletcher was feeling pretty heavily loaded with the suitcase, the holdall and the camera case slung over his shoulder.

" My God," Leonora said; " did you have to bring all that lot?"

" They're my things. I need them."

" Okay," she said, " okay, so you need them. Maybe we should have brought a truck."

He could tell that she was on edge, though she was doing her best to conceal her nervousness. When they came to the fence they both had reason to be nervous. King was not there.

They climbed over the fence and Leonora called his name softly : " Matthew! Where are you?"

There was no answer.

" We'd better make for the boat," she said. " Maybe he decided to go on ahead."

Fletcher could see no reason why King should do that, but there was no point in discussing the matter, and it would have been futile to hunt for him in the darkness. He glanced back at the bungalow. There was still plenty of light shining from it, but Joby was not following them. Fletcher had not expected him to.

" All right," he said. " Let's go."

He took the lead again, since he was more familiar with the way, and he had not gone more than twenty yards when he tripped over some obstacle lying in his path. He stumbled forward and nearly fell, dropping the bags. The obstacle was the body of a man.

The girl had come up close behind him and he could detect that edginess in her voice again.

" What is it, John? What's happened?"

Fletcher had turned. " I'm not sure," he said, " but I think we may have found Matthew."

" Oh God, no !" she said.

Fletcher pulled the small torch from his pocket and switched it on. The body revealed in the beam of the torch was that of a man lying face downward; but it was certainly not King. This man was wearing uniform.

" A cop !" Leonora said. " So where's Matthew?"

He answered for himself, appearing like a shadow out of the darkness. " I'm here. Switch the light off, John. You want to bring everybody running?"

Fletcher switched off the torch and put it back in his pocket. " What's been going on?"

" The cop came snooping round. I had to deal with him. I've been looking for any pals he might have had. There's a car down the road. One man in it. Asleep."

" Did you kill this one?" Fletcher asked.

" Don't think so. Just put him to sleep too. We better be moving."

" You don't think he may wake up and follow us?"

" When he wakes," King said, " he'll be in no state to follow anybody for quite a while. I used a rock."

" Maybe you used it a bit too hard."

" Maybe I did," King said. But it didn't seem to be bothering him. He picked up the holdall. " I'll carry this."

Fletcher was not sorry to be relieved of it; the suitcase was load enough. He led the way up the slope of the low ridge and down the other side, and a few minutes later they had passed through the belt of palm-trees and were on the beach.

" You took your time," Lawrence said. " Began to think I'd have to come looking for you."

" We had some trouble," Leonora said.

" Uh-huh! There's always trouble." Lawrence sounded unperturbed. " You get what you went for?"

" Yes," Fletcher said.

" That's okay, then. Everything's fine."

Fletcher was not sure he would have agreed. He was still worried about Joby and Paulina and the kids. He hoped the police would not harass them, but there was no telling about that. Perhaps they should have given Joby a bump on the head to prove that he had tried; but it would have taken more than that to convince the police, and they were going to be pretty angry when they found the man King had smacked with a rock; especially if the man was dead. They would not like that at all.

As the boat headed northward on the return trip he sat and pondered gloomily on the situation. He had really got himself into something now; and he could see no way out of it; no way at all.

" You're very silent," Leonora said. " What's on your mind?"

" Plenty of things," he said; " but most especially that I'm in the devil's own mess and it looks like staying that way."

" All life's a mess. We just have to make the best of it."

" And what's the best of this? You'd better tell me, because I'm damned if I can work it out for myself."

She leaned towards him in the darkness, and he felt the soft pressure of her lips.

" That?" he asked.

" It could be," she said. " It just could be."

*   *   *

It was still dark when they slipped the boat into its place between the other boats and made the rope fast to the post on the board-walk. The car was where they had left it and there was not a soul about at that hour in the morning. Leonora had the keys, but she handed them to King.

" You can drive, Matthew. I'm tired."

He took the keys without a word and unlocked the car. Fletcher stowed his luggage in the boot and heard Lawrence ask Leonora whether she would like to ride in the front. She said no; he could; she would rather sit in the back. She climbed in, and Fletcher got in on the other side. And then King started the engine and they were on their way.

A little while later she had snuggled up close to him

and he had his arm round her. Her head was resting on his shoulder, and it was not much longer before she was asleep. It was nice having her there like that; it was snug and warm and cosy, and he liked it that way. When he came to think about it, it seemed to be just about the nicest part of the whole damned business.

TEN

THE RIGHT PRICE

" You'd all better get some sleep now," Denning said.
" You've had a busy night and I imagine you're tired."

He had already been up and dressed when they arrived
back at the house, and they had had breakfast together.
Over breakfast they had given a report on the success of
the operation. Denning had listened with interest, putting
in a question now and then. On the whole he seemed to be
very well satisfied with the way things had gone, merely
remarking that the incident involving the policeman was
unfortunate, but something that could not be helped.

" It was only to be expected that they would keep a
watch on the place. But no matter; you have the camera
now, and there is nothing to prevent you taking a new set
of photographs."

" When ?" Fletcher asked.

Denning thought about it for a moment; then said :
" Tomorrow."

" Why not today?" King said. " Why not this afternoon?"

Denning shook his head. " No. I think it will be better to
leave it until tomorrow."

" That will be Saturday."

" It doesn't matter. What difference does it make what day of the week it is?"

King shrugged. " No difference, I guess. Okay, so it's tomorrow."

" I have to go into Jamestown this morning," Denning said. " We can talk over the final arrangements when I get back. Is that all right?"

Nobody raised any objections. Fletcher reflected that he was probably the only one who had any; and he objected to the entire scheme. But he had become resigned to it; all he wanted now was to get it over and done with.

" What about the aqualung?"

" I'll pick one up in Jamestown," Denning said. " You don't have to worry about that."

It was nice to know there was something he didn't have to worry about. There were plenty of things that were worrying the life out of him.

" Don't you think it's time I was told what this is all about?" he said. " I'm involved now, and I'd say I have a right to know what it is I'm involved in."

He received unexpected support from Leonora. " I agree." She looked at Denning. " What harm can it do? He's not going to the police; not when they want him on a murder charge. You yourself said he's with us now; so I say he ought to know what he's with us for."

Denning appeared uncertain, but finally he seemed to come to the conclusion that she was right. " Very well; you tell him. But wait until you've had that sleep. It'll keep until then."

*   *   *

Fletcher was on the balcony outside his bedroom when Denning drove away. He watched the Aston Martin until it was out of sight, then undressed and got into bed. But tired though he was, he found it impossible to sleep. His brain was too active; it was like a piece of clockwork that had been fully wound up and was going to take a long time to run down. After a couple of hours he gave it up. He shaved, had a shower, put on a shirt and a pair of cotton slacks, and went downstairs.

He found Leonora reclining on a long canvas chair on the terrace and reading a book.

" You too?" he said.

She put the book down and looked up at him. She was wearing sun-glasses with enormous frames.

" Me too?"

" Unable to sleep."

" It's the wrong time of day. Besides, I had some sleep in the car."

" So I recall." He pulled up another chair and sat down beside her. " Maybe you'd like to tell me now."

" About what goes on?"

" Yes."

She put a finger to her chin and seemed to think about it. " It's hard to know where to begin."

" How about the beginning?"

" Yes; but where was the beginning? You could go back years and years. You were right, of course; it is political."

" And Denning is trying to get into power?"

" Oh, no; it's not like that. Frankly, I don't think he cares two cents about that side of it. I suppose if things go right he might have some government post if he wants it;

but I'm sure that's not what he's working for. What he's doing is more disinterested; you could even say altruistic."

" And what is he doing?"

" He's the co-ordinator."

" I don't understand," Fletcher said. " The co-ordinator of what?"

" Of the resistance groups, freedom fighters, guerrillas, revolutionaries—call them what you like. They're scattered around the island; some in the mountains, some in the towns, some in the villages or on the estates. The groups vary in size; some are quite large, others very small; and the only link between them is here; this is the nerve-centre, where all the strategy is planned and—well—co-ordinated."

" And they come here?"

" The leaders do occasionally, but as seldom as possible. There are safer ways of contacting them."

" And Denning gets away with this? The police don't suspect him?"

" Why should they? He's very careful. To all outward appearances he's just a successful lawyer doing his job and enjoying the good things of life. Nobody would connect him with the revolutionary movement."

Fletcher let it sink in. He was not entirely surprised; he had suspected it must be something like this. But what he was not altogether convinced about was Denning's dis-interestedness, his altruism; it did not fit in with his own impression of the man; he would have said that Denning was very much interested in grasping power for himself and that this was the way he was going about it. To him the guerrillas were probably no more than a means to an end. But he did not put this suggestion to the girl; there was no

point in arguing about Denning's motives. And Denning
himself might eventually discover that he had miscalculated;
he might find the tool he had used turning in his hand. If
the revolutionaries ever did seize power they might choose
an altogether different kind of leader and thrust the elegant,
wealthy lawyer aside.

" And how," he asked, " did you become involved?"

" I came to write a story."

" No kidding?"

She smiled. " No kidding. It's like I told you; I'm a
journalist. Freelance at present."

" And you just decided that this was a good place to
come and find a story? Just like that?"

She must have been aware of his disbelief; it would
hardly have been possible not to be.

" There was a bit more to it than that."

" Tell me," he said. " We're not pressed for time."

She eased up the sun-glasses with her finger and scratched
the bridge of her nose; then lowered them again. He preferred her without the glasses; they covered too much of
her face, and he liked to see it all.

" All right," she said; " it was because of Matthew."

He was not sure he liked the sound of that. " In what
way?"

" We went to the same university back in the States. Not
one of the classy places; not one you'll ever have heard of.
Redmond, in Illinois. He was there on some kind of grant.
We got to be friendly; had a mutual interest in politics;
were both leftish."

" You mean communist?"

" No; I wouldn't say that. One can be left without being
Red. Anyway, when he came back home we used to write

to each other. Then he suggested I should come and do a magazine feature on the island's political set-up. He said he could introduce me to some interesting people. Which, of course, he could."

" So you came; and instead of writing a story you took a hand in the card-game?"

" Roughly speaking, yes."

" Why?"

" I don't really know." She sounded genuinely puzzled by her own motives. " It just seemed to happen that way."

Fletcher found himself looking at her legs. She was wearing a pair of shorts which ended just about where her thighs began, and the legs were a deep golden brown. Reluctantly he dragged his gaze away from this enchanting prospect.

" Are you in love with him?" he asked.

" With Matthew?" She sounded lazily amused. " No; it's nothing like that."

" He could be in love with you."

She shook her head. " No; he's dedicated to the cause."

" Nobody is ever that dedicated."

" Perhaps not. Would it bother you if he was in love with me?" There was still that faintly amused note in her voice.

" No," Fletcher said. " It would only bother me if you were in love with him."

She gave him a long, probing look through the monster sun-glasses. " Perhaps," she said, " we'd better not pursue that line of inquiry any further at this particular moment in time. It doesn't really have any bearing on the subject we were discussing, does it?"

" Perhaps not. So we'll just leave it on the table for the present. Now tell me about the Spanish Hawk."

" The Spanish Hawk?"

" The *Halcón Español.* The boat that was sunk. The boat with five dead men in it. Where does that fit into the picture? Why is everybody so interested in it?"

" Perhaps if I tell you where it came from you'll begin to guess. It came from Cuba."

Fletcher did begin to guess. But the fact that the boat had come from Cuba still left a lot to be explained.

" And the men in it?"

" Three Cubans. Two from this island."

Fletcher nodded. Ideas were taking form in his mind.

" And who killed them? Who sank the boat?"

" We can only make conjectures about that. The President's agents, undoubtedly; or the C.I.A. A combination of forces, possibly. What is reasonably certain is that the C.I.A., even if they took no active part, were pretty deeply involved in the affair."

" Now," Fletcher said, " you must give me some reasons. Why was this boat with these three Cubans and two islanders on board in this area?"

" It was heading for the island, of course, in order to put the men ashore."

" Secretly?"

" Yes. By night."

" Ah! And for what purpose were they going ashore? To give aid to the revolutionary movement, perhaps?"

" Naturally. The men from Cuba were experts in various aspects of guerrilla tactics. One of them was Carlos Maria Galeano."

She paused, as though expecting some remark.

" Is that name supposed to mean something to me?"
Fletcher asked.

" Carlos Maria Galeano was one of Castro's lieutenants
in the revolution, and a close friend."

" I see."

" That's why the C.I.A. wouldn't want the affair made
public. Because of possible reaction in Cuba."

" I don't quite get that. I should have said they wouldn't
give a damn about reactions in Cuba."

" And there you'd be wrong. Don't you know that it's the
policy of the present United States Government to do its
best to patch up relations with Cuba? Now what effect do
you imagine the revelation that Galeano and two other
important Cubans had been murdered by the C.I.A., or at
their instigation, would have on any possible détente between the two countries? It would be disastrous. Now do
you see how important those photographs are?"

" But surely the Cuban Government will get to know
about what happened anyway. It's bound to leak out."

" Possibly. But they may choose to ignore such vague
reports; to gloss the thing over. After all, it's to their
advantage as well to improve relations with the States. But
if photographs and a full account of the incident were to be
published, it would hardly be possible for them to ignore
the matter, would it?"

" I don't see why that should bother President Rodgers.
What does he stand to lose?"

" Anything that bothers the C.I.A. bothers Clayton
Rodgers. He's on their pay-roll."

" Ah, of course."

" It's my opinion—and here I'm only guessing, mind—
that in this instance the C.I.A. rather over-reached them-

selves and are in trouble back home. So they'll do their damnedest to cover up what may have been a blunder from the diplomatic point of view. Hence the attempt to bribe you to clear out."

" I was a fool not to accept the offer."

" Maybe you were. Frankly, I think you're lucky to be still alive and kicking. I don't know why they bothered with trying to buy you off; I'd have expected them just to eliminate you. They're not noted for being squeamish when they see an obstacle in their way."

" Perhaps it had something to do with my nationality. The U.K. and the U.S. are supposed to be allies, aren't they? Nato and all that."

Her smile was a trifle grim. " If I were you, John, I wouldn't rely too heavily on that consideration to hold them in check. You're safer with us, believe you me."

It might have been so, but he did not feel safe; there were too many people looking for him and ready to do him an injury.

" It's a funny thing," she said, " but if you hadn't taken those photos we might never have known what happened to the boat. All we knew until then was that it failed to arrive at the rendezvous. And even then we might still have known nothing if you hadn't trusted the film to Dharam Singh, and if he hadn't spotted the chance of a bit of quick profit by selling the prints."

" Yes," Fletcher said, " that was a daft thing to do— letting him have the film, I mean. I should have known he would hang on to some copies. I suppose it was the editor of *Freedom* who let you know about them?"

" Yes. Actually, he didn't know the inside story, but he thought he recognised some of the dead men and he made a pretty shrewd guess at what had happened. He was very excited about it, poor devil."

" Why poor devil?"

" Didn't you know? He's dead. They shot him. Resisting arrest. Anyway, before that happened Matthew went along to the place and had a look at the pictures, and of course he saw at once what they were."

" He was lucky not to be there when the police raided the press. Where was it?"

" In a cellar in Jamestown, under a laundry. But Matthew was well clear before the police moved in."

" Why didn't he bring away some copies of the photographs?"

" At that time there was only the one set. They hadn't got to work on them."

Fletcher was silent for a while, chewing it over. Then he said: " What I don't understand is why the guerrillas should be so keen to publish the photographs. What can they hope to gain by it?"

" Nothing directly, perhaps. But anything that might embarrass Clayton Rodgers is grist to their mill. And besides, they're not exactly keen on the idea of any recon-ciliation between Havana and Washington. You have to remember also that two of their top men were killed. That in itself would be enough to make them pretty bitter; they wouldn't need any more logical reason."

" I suppose not."

Again they were silent. The magnificent landscape stretched away on all sides; a few white clouds floated around, but no rain threatened. Somewhere a gardener was singing at his work, and the song mingled with the faint sounding of water tumbling over rocks. Fletcher reflected

that Conrad Denning had it made: with all this, why
should he take the risk of sticking his fingers into the revolutionary pie? Why was he not content with what he had?
But some men were never content.

"Is Denning married?" he asked.

Leonora turned her head lazily. "Divorced."

"Any children?"

"I believe the wife has custody of them."

"Have you met her?"

"No."

"So he has no family ties?"

"None at all, as far as I know. He's not exactly the
family man type. Too many other interests."

"And he could lose everything."

"How do you mean?" she asked.

"If Clayton Rodgers ever gets to hear of what his dear
cousin is doing, that'll be the end of it."

"How should he get to hear about it?"

"How did he get to hear about the boat? How did he
get to hear about the photographs? Somebody must be
feeding him information; somebody who's in the know.
Somewhere in the ranks there's an informer. Have you
thought about that?"

She frowned. "Of course I've thought about it."

"And have you come up with anything? How many
people knew about the Spanish Hawk operation?"

"I don't know. Quite a number, I imagine."

"Including you?"

She looked startled. "Are you suggesting I might have
been the informer?"

"No," Fletcher said. "What motive would you have for
betraying your friends?"

But the thought had crossed his mind, nevertheless; because money was always a pretty good motive in any language, if there was enough of it.

It seemed as if she had been thinking along somewhat parallel lines, for a moment or two later she said musingly : " Though if it comes to the point just about anyone can be bought if the price is right. It's all a question of finding the right price."

" Well, it looks as though they found the right price for someone," Fletcher said. And he was wondering just how safe he was at Denning's place after all; how safe he was going to be diving from Denning's boat to take more pictures of the wreck; how safe he was anywhere with this lot. Because whoever had passed the information regarding the *Halcón Español* and the *Freedom* press might even now be passing more information—with his name mixed up in it.

" What are you thinking about now?" Leonora asked.

" Hatchet men," Fletcher said.

*   *   *

Denning returned in the middle of the afternoon. He looked cheerful, like a man who feels that things are running his way. Fletcher wished that he himself had been feeling half as cheerful as Denning looked, and he felt resentful about it. Denning had the aqualung in the boot of the Aston Martin, and showed it to Fletcher.

" I hope it will be all right."

" I don't see why it shouldn't be," Fletcher said. " As long as they haven't put chlorine in the cylinders."

Denning must have detected a note of sourness. " You don't appear to have slept too well."

" I haven't slept at all. I listened to a long story instead. It was pretty sordid in places."

" You've been talking to Leonora?"

" Yes."

" And now you know it all?"

" And I don't like it."

" You're not being asked to like it." Denning's voice had hardened slightly and he seemed a shade less genial. " Just do the job, that's all."

" And after?"

" We'll have to think about that, won't we?"

" I have thought about it."

" And?"

" And I want a boat to take me off the island."

" Where do you propose to go?"

" I'm not much bothered. Anywhere in the Caribbean from which I can get a flight or a sea passage back to England."

" We'll have to see about that."

" Yes," Fletcher said, " you see about it. And don't take too long seeing about it, either, because I'm not terribly keen on the idea of being taken home in a coffin."

Denning gave a laugh; he seemed to think it was a good joke. Fletcher was damned if he could see anything funny in it, so maybe he was standing in the wrong place.

" Well," Denning said, " I'm sure we shall be able to work something out. But tomorrow we have another problem on our minds. Tomorrow you have a bit of underwater photography to do. I expect you're looking forward to it."

" Like a man looks forward to having both legs amputated."

Denning laughed again. Fletcher thought he had never met anyone with such a warped sense of humour.

ELEVEN

TOUCH WOOD

They rose early and drove to the village before daybreak. It was still not light when they went on board the boat and eased it out of its berth. Denning himself had arranged for it to be refuelled the previous day and the tanks were full. A few minutes later they had cleared the harbour and were heading east.

It was too good a start—no snags, no hitches, no inquisitive officials, no policemen, nothing. Fletcher could not believe that the whole operation would go as smoothly as this. It was simply too good to last.

Lawrence again was at the helm. Fletcher was sitting on one side of the cockpit and King was hunched up on the opposite side, looking cold. The air was fresh and cool, and the sea was calm. The boat was running smoothly at an easy speed and Lawrence was not pushing it; there was plenty of time.

Leonora had driven them down to the harbour and Fletcher had sat beside her in the front of the car. They had talked off and on, and he had asked her how Denning was going to spend the day.

" I don't know," she said. " Does it matter?"

Fletcher could see no reason why she should have come

with them; any one of them could have driven the Ford, and they could have parked it where they had left it before. It meant an extra journey, because she would have to come and meet them when they returned; but perhaps she liked driving.

" No," he said; " it doesn't matter. He can just sit around at Mission Control and wait for the boys to come back. Nice for him."

She gave him a quick glance. " You don't like Conrad, do you?"

" Am I supposed to like him?"

" Not if you don't want to."

" Do you like him?"

" Yes," she said, " I do."

He wondered, with a sudden stab of jealousy, whether there was anything between Denning and her. She had been living for quite a while in his house, so there had been ample opportunity. And Denning was a handsome devil, no doubt about that; mature certainly, but nevertheless handsome; the kind of man a girl half his age might very well fall for. So had she fallen for him? Though he had asked her whether she was in love with Matthew King, he hesitated to ask a similar question in this instance. And why? Because he feared what the answer might be? Maybe, damn it. Yes; maybe so.

She must have sensed that something was wrong. " What's on your mind?" she asked. " Is it the job? Is that what's bothering you?"

" You bet it's bothering me," he said. " It scares me sick."

" The diving?"

" No, not that. I do that for fun."

" What is it, then?"

" I keep thinking when the thing's done there may be a reception committee waiting for us."

" That's crazy. Nobody knows—"

" Nobody knew about the boat coming from Cuba. Remember?"

" That was different."

" You mean there were more people in the secret?"

" Yes."

" Okay; so this time there aren't so many. But as long as you just have two people in a secret, it isn't a secret any more."

" You really do worry too much," she said.

" Yes, maybe I do," Fletcher agreed. But he had a feeling that now he was not alone; perhaps he had her worrying too.

She had helped them get the gear on board and had watched as the boat moved out of the berth. Fletcher's last sight of her was a lone figure standing under the lamp on the board-walk; looking somehow a little forlorn and dejected, he thought. But he could think of no reason why she should have been; unless she had been thinking about what he had said. And wondering.

When it grew light they were already out of sight of land. Lawrence altered course a few points to the southward and kept the boat going at the same steady rate of knots, since there was no need for haste; they would be at the right place soon enough.

King said: " You got the camera all fixed up ready?"

" I've got it fixed up," Fletcher said.

" Soon be there now."

Fletcher grunted.

" Anybody like some coffee?" King asked. He had brought a big vacuum flask and sandwiches.

They all had coffee. The sandwiches had chicken and ham in them. Fletcher ate two. Physically he felt better for the snack; mentally he was in the same depressed state. It grew steadily warmer as the sun rose; the sea gleamed as though the surface had been strewn with silver plates; an oil-tanker, made small by distance, appeared to be utterly motionless on the skyline, but a little later when Fletcher looked for it, it had vanished.

The rocky islet appeared out of the haze ahead, gradually becoming clearer. To the east of it was another, smaller object. Fletcher was the first to spot it.

" There's a boat."

" Damn !" King said.

Fletcher did not care for the look of it; the other boat seemed to be just about at the place where the wreck was, a short way to the east of the islet. It was as though it had been waiting for them.

" I think we're in trouble."

" You're jumping to conclusions," Lawrence said. " Just because there's a boat don't mean it has to have anything to do with us."

" It's a bit of a coincidence it should be right there. Wouldn't you say it was? It doesn't seem to be moving."

" How can you tell? It's too far away."

King picked up a pair of powerful binoculars, focused them on the other boat and studied it intently for a while. Then he handed the binoculars to Fletcher.

" Take a look."

Fletcher put the binoculars to his eyes and the distance separating the two boats seemed to contract miraculously.

The one ahead appeared to be a large motor-launch and he could see some men moving about on board. And then he saw a sudden flurry of foam at the stern, and he half expected the launch to turn about and start heading towards them; but it did not. In fact, it appeared to be heading in the opposite direction, the white break of water at the bows indicating that it was building up a good turn of speed.

" They're going away."

" You see," Lawrence said. " There wasn't nothing to worry about. They're not interested in us."

" So I was wrong. But they might have been."

Lawrence did not contradict him, and he guessed that the man had had his own misgivings, even though he might not have confessed to any. He had a feeling that all three of them were relieved to see the launch heading away from them.

Lawrence reduced speed to allow it to get well clear, and by the time they reached the area where the wreck was submerged it had vanished into the haze on the southern horizon. There was now not another boat in sight, and things still could not have been going more smoothly.

" We're going to be lucky," King said. " I feel it in my bones. We sure are going to be lucky."

Fletcher touched wood; there was plenty of it within reach. He still did not trust that luck to last. When had it ever done so?

*　　　*　　　*

They had got the bearings almost dead accurate. When he had swum down through those ten fathoms of clear sea-water he could see the stern of the ship ahead of him, and that old four-inch breech-loader which had fired its last round so many years ago. The gun was mounted on a platform above the poop, a kind of metallic mushroom growth springing out of the deck; the barrel, at right angles to the line of the masts, was a thick finger pointing at the ocean bed, as though directing the attention to some object lying there; the breech was closed, just as the last Number Two of the gun crew had left it; the elevating and training wheels were motionless and would remain so perhaps for ever.

Fletcher swam towards the ship and stopped at the stern, one hand resting lightly on the taffrail. Utter silence; utter stillness; even the fishes seemed to have deserted the wreck for the moment. Fletcher could not see the boat from that position; the *Halcón Español* was hidden by the midships superstructure; but he knew it was there, less than a ship's length away, waiting for him to come to it.

And the dead men waiting, too.

And suddenly he had no wish to go to it or to them. What would they be like now? Bloated, repulsive, horrifying. Was he to photograph such things? He felt cold, as if the thought had chilled his blood. Why should he do it? What good would it do? Suppose he returned to the surface and reported that he had been unable to find the ship. What could they do? They could not prove that he was lying.

Still he waited there with his hand on the rail, and still the fishes had not returned to the ship. And gradually, insidiously, there crept over him a sense of impending disaster. Something was about to happen; he was sure of it. And perhaps the fishes had also felt that premonition; perhaps that was why they had gone. So he would take an

example from them and would go too; would get away
from that place where evil seemed to be lying in wait like a
dreaded spectre.

He took his hand off the taffrail and was about to thrust
away from the poop when it happened. The entire ship
trembled and moved, as though the long sleep had ended
and now she would lift herself off the bed of the sea, rise to
the surface and go steaming on as she had done throughout
those early years of the century. But it was no more than a
spasm; the movement was not sustained, and she subsided
again while a mass of débris that had exploded from the
region of the foredeck—pieces of timber, iron, wire-rope,
brass and copper, all mixed up with sediment from the
ocean floor—rose like a dark and awful cloud.

Fletcher stared at it, not moving, petrified by the sight.
He had had that premonition of something about to happen, but he had not dreamed that it would be this. And
now he knew for what purpose the launch had been there:
divers had been down from it to fix the charge and the
timing device; and they must have just completed the task
when the second boat hove in sight. That was why they had
gone away so quickly; their work had been finished and
they had no further reason for hanging around.

These thoughts flitted through his mind in the instant
when the explosion occurred, and a moment later he was
caught by the pressure of water and it was as though an
invisible, irresistible force were carrying him away. He
made no attempt to resist it, but allowed himself to be
thrust forward until the pressure eased. Then he swam back
to the ship and looked at the damage.

They had made a thorough job of it: the boat had
disintegrated and there was nothing now that could have

been identified as part of it; the *Halcón Español* no longer existed. As to the bodies, there were objects here and there which might have been parts of a man, but soon they would be gone and there would be nothing; nothing at all to give evidence of the killing that had taken place; nothing that would be worth the expenditure of one millimetre of photographic film.

The ship had sustained some more damage to go with that meted out by the torpedo so many years ago, but this extra injury was of no importance; a sunken vessel could be sunk no deeper. She had stirred for a moment and that was all; now she would lie once again undisturbed, and the fishes would come back to dart and flicker between the holds and superstructure while time stood still. He turned away from the wreckage and began to swim towards the surface.

*   *   *

He could tell by their faces that they knew something had gone wrong. They helped him to climb on board; they helped him to get rid of the mask and the cylinders and the camera.

It was King who asked the question that must have been in the minds of both.

" What happened?"

He told them. They were not surprised; the explosion had been noticeable on the surface; pieces of flotsam had come up and were floating around the boat.

" You're lucky to be alive," King said. " You were so long coming up, we began to think—"

" That I'd copped it? If I'd gone in straightaway I should have done. But I hung back, not liking it. That's what saved me—blue funk."

" I'm glad it did." King grinned at him. " We'd have hated to lose you."

" I'd have hated it too."

" So they decided to destroy the evidence," King said. " Well, it was to be expected. It was the easiest way. We were just too late; we should have come yesterday."

" If we'd come yesterday," Fletcher said, " maybe they would have been here yesterday instead."

King gave him a quick glance. " You're saying they were warned? That they knew what we planned?"

" I don't know. But it's a coincidence, isn't it? Like I said before. And me, I just don't believe in coincidences."

" Well, well," King said; " now we have got something to think about."

It was Lawrence who broke in then. " Think about it on the way back. I say we better get the hell outa here right now."

" Okay; let's go."

Fletcher had been looking towards the islet. Now he suddenly pointed.

" Look there!"

" Hell!" Lawrence said.

A motor-launch had come into view and was approaching rapidly. Until then it had been hidden by the islet, but now it had come out into the open and was heading directly for the smaller boat.

" The bastards!" King said. " They came back."

It was possible. It could have been the launch they had seen going away as they approached. It could have gone out of sight, then changed direction, made a detour, and returned under cover of the islet. On the other hand, this might be a different launch, one that had been lurking there all the time. Either way, it made no difference; the odds were a hundred to one that it was not approaching simply to pass the time of day.

" Get this thing moving," King said urgently.

Lawrence needed no goading; he was already trying to start the engine and was having trouble. It was a fine time for the engine to turn temperamental. The launch was whittling away the distance between the two boats with every moment that passed.

" For God's sake," King said, " what's wrong with it?" He was edgy, reminding Fletcher of the way he had been that first evening of their acquaintance in the Treasure Ship. Perhaps he had had reason to be edgy then; he certainly had reason now. " For God's sake, Lawrence !"

Lawrence snarled something back at him that was about as obscene as you could get in half a dozen words, and he sounded edgy too. The engine gave a brief splutter and died again.

Fletcher picked up the binoculars and trained them on the launch. He saw that a man had climbed on to the roof of the cabin and was lying down with what appeared to be a submachine-gun in his hands. Things were beginning to look very unpleasant indeed. He put the binoculars down and glanced at King; there was an automatic pistol in King's hand, but if it came to a shooting match the odds were on the submachine-gun.

Suddenly the engine gave a cough and really came to life, and it was one of the most welcome sounds Fletcher had heard in quite some time. There was a swirl of water at the stern and the boat began to move.

" Well, thanks be for that," King muttered. " Thanks be for that."

But the launch was still overhauling them and the gap was shrinking with each second that passed. Suddenly the man who was lying on the cabin-top, apparently judging the range to be short enough, let go with the submachine-gun. Bullets flicked the surface of the water just astern of the boat, flinging up little fountains of spray.

" Get down," King shouted.

He could have saved his breath; the man with the sub-machine-gun had done all the persuading that was needed. Fletcher dropped quickly to the bottom of the cockpit and was joined there by King. Only Lawrence, who was steering, remained on his feet; he had to keep the boat under control. King got up on to his knees and did some work with the pistol, but he might as well have thrown the gun itself for all the effect it was likely to have; there was not one chance in a million of hitting anyone in the launch.

By now the boat was gathering speed and the launch was no longer gaining on it. Gradually they began to draw away from the pursuer.

" Good boy, Lawrence," King said. " That's the way. Keep her going."

The man with the submachine-gun was still firing in short bursts, but he was in little better situation than King for accurate shooting; at the speed it was moving the launch provided a very unstable platform, and with the range beginning to open again the chances of scoring a telling hit were rapidly fading.

There came a lull. Fletcher raised his head and peered over the stern. He could see the man doing something with the gun, probably changing the magazine. The distance between the boats was looking much healthier and it was apparent that theirs was the faster of the two. Barring accidents, like a breakdown of the engine, it looked as though they were going to make it.

Another sudden burst of fire made him duck his head again; the man on the cabin-top had obviously got the new magazine fixed and there was no sense in taking unnecessary risks even if the range had increased. King had evidently come to the conclusion that pistol work was useless and had stowed the automatic away. Fletcher looked at him and grinned.

" They won't catch us now. This is a fast boat."

Perhaps he ought to have been touching wood again. At that moment there was another, longer burst of fire from the submachine-gun, as though the operator had decided to give it one last try, and some splinters of wood were chipped off the stern of the boat. Lawrence gave a cry of pain and staggered sideways, dragging at the wheel as he fell, so that the boat heeled sharply over and came round in a wide sweep to starboard. A little more and it might have made a complete turn if King had not realised the danger and grabbed the wheel to bring it back on course.

The submachine-gun was still firing spasmodically, but it stopped abruptly and Fletcher guessed that the second magazine had been emptied. He peered over the stern and saw that the involuntary manoeuvre of the boat had lost them some of their lead. But already the gap was widening again.

He went to help Lawrence, who was sitting on the bottom of the cockpit with his back propped up against the side. Apparently he had been hit in the left arm; he was wearing a short-sleeved shirt and there was blood dripping from the area of the bicep muscle. The entire lower arm was in a mess, but it probably looked worse than it was.

The submachine-gun really seemed to have gone out of business this time. He glanced again across the gap of water and saw that the launch had slipped even further astern; it was no longer in the hunt and they could forget about any more danger from the gun. He felt considerable relief at that; it was the first time in his life that he had been shot at, and he had not enjoyed the experience. He hoped it would be the last time also, but in the circumstances he would not have been prepared to lay a very heavy bet on that particular horse.

He turned again to Lawrence. " How bad is it?"

Lawrence looked pretty sick, but he managed a grin. Or it might have been a grimace; it was hard to tell.

" I'll live," he said.

" I hope we all shall," Fletcher said. But he was afraid it might be tough going.

TWELVE

SOME GIRL

'They took the boat into a small creek on the northern side of the island. King knew the place and he said it would be safe enough there. It was pretty secluded and not easy to get at; there was no road leading to it.

" We shall have to make it back to the house the best way we can."

It had been obvious that it would not be safe to return to their starting point; they would almost certainly have found the police waiting for them. So they had headed north and then west, keeping well out to sea until the time had come to turn south and make a dash for the coast. There had always been the possibility that, warned by radio, another boat might have been sent out to intercept them, or even a helicopter; but in the event there had been nothing to give them any cause for alarm. They had seen other boats—yachts and motor-launches—but none that had appeared to be attempting any interception, and the trip had been without further incident.

Fletcher had put a dressing on Lawrence's arm, using bandages from the boat's first-aid kit, and had succeeded in stemming the flow of blood. It seemed that the bullet had passed completely through the flesh without touching a bone. He had made a sling for the arm and Lawrence seemed to be reasonably comfortable, though he was obviously in some pain.

None of them was happy with the way things had gone. They had all smelled the odour of treachery and it was not the kind of odour that anyone liked. The question that arose and was discussed at some length on the way back was: who had betrayed them?

It was Fletcher who touched on the nub of the matter. "Who knew about this operation? The three of us and Conrad Denning and Leonora. That's five. Who else?"

"No one else," King said, not looking round, just gripping the wheel hard and staring straight ahead past the bows of the boat.

"We don't know that," Lawrence objected. "Not for certain. There could have been someone else."

"How could there have been?" Fletcher asked.

"Someone else could have been told."

"Well, that's precisely what we're talking about, isn't it? Who told someone else? Did you? Did Matthew? Did I?"

None of them had spoken about it to anyone; they were adamant on that.

"So who does that leave?"

It left two people—Denning and the girl.

They were all silent, thinking about it; then King said slowly: "I don't believe it. She wouldn't."

"How do you know she wouldn't?"

"I know her. I've known her since way back."

Lawrence said thoughtfully: "I wonder. Do we ever know anybody? Like really know them."

"She wouldn't," King said; and he still was not

looking round; it was as though he was afraid to meet their eyes.

Fletcher could see how it was: King did not want to believe that Leonora would betray them. And if it came to that, he himself did not want to believe it, either. But the logic was too strong; it all added up; and the more he thought about it, the more obvious it seemed. She could have been feeding information to the C.I.A. all along. She was an American, so what more likely? She might even be a C.I.A. agent herself.

" I was the one who invited her here," King said. Which was true, but proved nothing. " So why would she do it?"

" People do a lotta things for money," Lawrence said. " It's got a strong, strong pull, that old money."

" She doesn't want money."

" Ain't nobody don't want money," Lawrence said.

" I don't believe it. I just don't believe it."

" So why didn't she come with us? Like last time when we went for the camera. She came then."

" There was no need for her to come."

" There was no need then, but she came."

" It's not proof."

" Oh, sure it's not proof. But you just think back a while. Who knew about that other boat coming from Cuba? Who knew about the pictures in *Freedom*? And other things; other times when the cops moved in."

" She was never the only one who knew."

" But she did know, and she knew about us today."

Fletcher was silent. He wished he could have said something in the girl's defence, but it would only have been an attempt to fool himself. He remembered what she had said to him when they had talked the thing over on Denning's terrace. She had said: "Are you suggesting I might have been the informer?" He had denied it, but he had had his doubts even then. Now he knew. And he knew, too, that what really hurt was the realisation that she had been willing to betray him as well as the others. He remembered the way she had snuggled up to him in the back of the Ford and had gone to sleep with her head resting against his shoulder; and the way she had stood on the board-walk watching the boat move out that morning. He had begun to think she really had some feeling for him, the same as he had for her. And now this. It hurt; it hurt right down to the bone.

"Damn her!" King burst out suddenly. "Damn her! Damn her!" He beat his hand on the wheel as though it were the object of his anger; and Fletcher knew just how he was feeling. He knew that King also had accepted the bitter fact, and that it was the same with him, because he loved her too; you could bet your life he did.

"So what do we do about it?"

"We go back. She'll be there."

"And then?"

"We'll see," King said grimly. "We'll see."

*   *   *

It was a hard journey back to Denning's place on foot. Lawrence was not in the best of condition for travelling; his arm was still giving him pain, and he was forced to stop and rest from time to time in order to recover his strength. At first there was not even a road, and when they did at last come to one it meandered tantalisingly, seldom taking them for long in exactly the right direction; rough and dusty, undulating as a switchback, and fiendishly hard on the feet.

They had one piece of good fortune: an ancient lorry overtook them and stopped a short distance ahead. When they came up with it they found a skinny bone-bag of a driver leaning out of the cab and grinning at them.

" Hey, you wanna lift?"

On the other side of him was a woman fat enough to have made two of him, who was probably his wife.

" Thanks," King said. " It'd be better than walking."

The man looked at Lawrence. " You had an accident?"

" That's right," Lawrence said. " An accident."

" He broke his arm," King said.

The woman leaned across, squeezing the man up against the door, so that she could get a view of Lawrence.

" Man, you look sick. Like you need a doctor."

" I'm okay," Lawrence said.

" Don't look like you're okay; not to me, it don't. You bin bleedin' some."

It had taken no great powers of observation to discover that fact; the bandage on Lawrence's arm was dark with blood that had soaked through. He was sweating heavily and there was a kind of scum round his mouth; his breathing sounded laboured.

" I'm okay," he said again.

" Well, if you say so." The woman was unconvinced, but she was not going to argue about it.

" Where you heading?" the driver asked.

" Your way," King said.

The man nodded, his eyes keen and shrewd. " You bin in trouble mebbe?"

" A little. Does it bother you?"

The man shook his head, twisting the cords in the scraggy neck. " Don't bother me none. Jest so long as you don't bring none of that trouble with you."

" It's all behind us," King said.

Fletcher thought it was an optimistic statement. There could be quite a bag of trouble lying ahead. The skinny driver seemed to think so too, and for a moment there was a flicker of doubt in his eye, as though he might have been about to change his mind and cancel the offer of a lift. But then he made a gesture with his hand towards the back of the lorry.

" Okay. Climb up."

There were some crates and fruit trays and empty sacks in the back, which seemed to indicate that the man was making a return journey from an expedition to market in Jamestown or one of the seaside holiday resorts. King and Fletcher helped Lawrence climb on board and then followed him. The lorry had tall slatted sides which swayed crazily as it went over the pot-holes, and the engine hammered away relentlessly, complaining in a whining low gear on all the steeper gradients. They sat on the sacks with their legs stretched out and backs resting against the cab, watching the dust-clouds raised by the wheels like daylight phantoms which slowly disintegrated and vanished in the distance.

" You think she'll go down to meet the boat?" King said; revealing the subject that was occupying his mind.

" She'll have to go," Fletcher said. " How would she explain it to Denning if she didn't? But that doesn't mean she'll expect to see the boat come in."

" How long do you think she'll wait?"

" Long enough to make it look right. Then she'll go back

and report to Denning. No boat. She could be back already. It's getting late."

" He won't like it. We're his link-men, me and Lawrence. We keep him in touch. If he were to lose us it'd be hard for him to find replacements he could trust."

" How long has it been going on?" Fletcher asked. " I mean this co-ordinating arrangement."

" Three years. Maybe getting on for four."

" Whose idea was it?"

" His."

" And you trusted him?"

" Not at first. You don't trust a man like that straight off. You wait until you find out if he's to be trusted."

" How long did that take?"

" A year maybe. Been going good ever since."

" But there have been setbacks?"

" Oh, sure. Bound to be setbacks."

" When did Leonora join you?"

" Could be twelve months back."

" As long as that? Didn't it ever strike you as strange that she should hang on all that time, occupying herself with your revolutionary activities? Didn't you ever ask yourself why she took such an interest in something that didn't really concern her?"

King looked slightly embarrassed. " Maybe I did."

" And what answer did you come up with?"

" It doesn't matter."

Fletcher got the idea that King had not bothered too much with the answer. As long as Leonora was there, that had been enough for him. And perhaps she had given him enough encouragement sexually to keep him on the string. And had used the same method with Denning? He wondered just how far a dedicated C.I.A. agent would be prepared to go in the line of duty, and again he felt a stab of jealousy; even though he knew now what she was, how treacherous she could be, he could still feel jealous; it was illogical, but it was a fact. And she must have been clever; keeping both King and Denning nibbling at the same bait would have required no little skill, considerable discretion. High marks for Leonora. Some girl. Some bloody girl.

The shaking of the lorry was doing Lawrence no good at all; now and then he groaned a little. Even though it was long past its zenith, the sun was still hot, and he was sweating.

" How much further is it to Denning's house?" Fletcher asked.

" Five or six miles," King said. " Nearer in a straight line."

" But we don't travel in a straight line."

" No. Need wings for that."

The lorry came to a halt after about half an hour. Fletcher and King stood up and looked over the side. The driver was leaning out of his cab.

" This here's where I turn off. I got a place down there." He pointed to a rough track branching off to the right and overhung with trees. " Be out of your way, likely."

" Yes," King said, " it would. We'll get down here."

The woman thrust her head out. " You like some refreshment? You welcome. You look like you could all use a long cool drink."

King seemed about to refuse, but he glanced at Lawrence and must have seen how sick Lawrence was looking, and he hesitated.

" How far is it to your place?"

" Quarter of a mile," the skinny man said. " Mebbe more. It's outa your way." He seemed to be trying to put them off.

" You welcome," the woman said again.

Fletcher was not at all sure the man would have gone along with that; not all the way. But he did not contradict her.

" Well," King said, " maybe a long cool drink wouldn't be so bad at that."

The woman's head and then the man's disappeared. King and Fletcher sat down and the lorry got under way again, bumping off the road on to the track which would have been better suited to mules than to wheeled vehicles. The lorry stayed in low gear for the rest of the way, and they could hear the springs creaking and the boards complaining, so that it seemed as though the whole thing were about to break up into its component parts. But no doubt it had done that particular run a good many times, and maybe even worse runs, and it had not broken up yet, so it could have been that it was stronger than it looked in spite of its age; and after a few minutes of this bumpy progress it came again to a halt and they were there.

It was not much in the style of Denning's house. It was not very big; there was just the one storey; and it was built on sloping ground, so that one end had had to be propped up on stilts. It was made of rough planks that had never had a lick of paint or a plane on them from the moment when they had been sawn from the log, and the way they had warped showed that they had been used green. The roof was of corrugated-iron, rusting in places, and there was a veranda at the front end with steps leading up to it. There were some citrus trees and bananas, and patches of ground under rough cultivation, and there were half a dozen goats and some chickens scratching around.

Six children, ranging in age from maybe fourteen down to four, came running to meet the lorry, yelling with excitement and then falling suddenly silent when they caught sight of the three strangers. The man and the woman got out of the cab, and King and Fletcher helped Lawrence to get down from the back. The children stood bunched together, staring at them with wide eyes, as though they had been visitors from outer space.

Fletcher spoke to the woman. " Your family?"

She smiled proudly, nodding. " Every last one."

" Nice," Fletcher said. " Very nice."

It seemed to gratify her; she really beamed this time. " You like kids?"

" I love kids," Fletcher said.

She chuckled. " These here kids is little devils."

" I can't believe you mean that. They look like angels."

The children giggled. They didn't believe she meant it, either.

" You better come inside," the woman said.

They all went up the steps to the veranda and into the house, the children following, crowding in the doorway. It was the living-room; the furniture was old, worn, faded; there was a sofa with the springs thrusting up under the covering material like bones under the skin of a starved and mangy horse. Lawrence sat down and leaned back with a sigh of thankfulness.

" I go get them drinks," the woman said.

She went through a doorway into what was probably the kitchen and came back with three glasses on a tray. Fletcher took one; it was cool and it tasted like lime-juice with a dash of rum in it. Lawrence emptied his glass quickly and it seemed to do him a lot of good.

" You feel better now?" the woman asked.

Lawrence managed a grin. " Much better. You mix a good drink."

" You like another?"

" No more, thanks. We have to be on our way."

" No need to go yet. You better rest awhile."

Lawrence glanced at King.

King said. " Sure. Give it a bit of time. No hurry."

The skinny man looked as if he were wishing he had never stopped and offered them a lift; Fletcher could see that he was itching to be rid of them. Perhaps he thought that a man with a bloody bandage on his arm was not the kind to have around the place if you were looking for a quiet life. And he could have been right at that.

" Coupla hours it'll be dark," he said. " You figure you can make it to where you're going in that time without transport?"

" We're not afraid of the dark," King said.

" Well, it's you that's walking it." The skinny man turned and walked out of the house.

" Don't need to take no notice of him," the woman said. " He just don't like visitors."

" Maybe it depends on the visitors," King said.

Fletcher hoped that Lawrence would soon feel fit enough to make a move. He wanted to get back to Denning's place and thresh things out. But then it occurred to him that perhaps the police would be there waiting for them, and that was not at all a pleasant thought. It would be well to approach the house with caution.

The children had plucked up courage to come into the

room; they were no longer so overawed by the three strangers. The woman introduced them all by name. She said the skinny man's name was Bruce; she was Mrs. Bruce. She paused expectantly, waiting for the three of them to reveal their names, but no one did so. It seemed to disconcert her a little; her manner became perceptibly less friendly; but she did not ask them directly who they were.

Mr. Bruce came back and stared at them coldly. Fletcher felt uncomfortable, even more impatient to go. But Lawrence had his eyes closed and King was making no move. The eldest boy switched on a transistor radio and the room was filled with the sound of pop music. The boy and two of the girls began to sway to the rhythm, their young bodies moving as sinuously as snakes. The music had the effect of rousing Lawrence; he opened his eyes and sat up.

" We better go."

" If you're ready," King said.

Lawrence stood up, and Fletcher was relieved to see that the drink and the brief rest did indeed appear to have refreshed him. He looked now as though he might well be fit enough to walk the rest of the way.

" I'm ready."

The woman made no attempt to detain them this time; she seemed as happy to see them making ready to depart as her husband was.

The music broke off suddenly in mid-flow. There was a short silence, then a voice in which excitement and emotion were obvious trying to break through, so that it was only with difficulty kept under control, said:

" Here is an important announcement. A report has just come in that President Clayton Rodgers has been assassinated. It appears that six armed men got into the gardens of the Presidential Palace, shot their way past the guards, and killed the President in his private swimming-pool. Three of the assassins were shot by the guards, but the other three escaped. One of the men who escaped is believed to have been wounded, possibly in the arm."

THIRTEEN

CONFRONTATION

There was a sharp click. Mr. Bruce had stretched out his hand and switched off the radio. For a few moments nobody said a word; even the kids were silent. The man and the woman were staring at Lawrence, staring at the bandaged arm. Fletcher could read what was passing in their minds; it needed no gift of clairvoyance to do that. They could count up to three and they could draw conclusions.

It was King who finally broke the silence. " So he's dead. Well, he had it coming. Who's going to mourn him?"

Bruce said, his voice cracking slightly: " You better go now. We don't want you here. You better go."

" We're going," King said. He turned to the woman. " Thanks for the refreshment."

She stared at him with frightened eyes, as though half expecting him to pull out a gun and shoot her where she stood.

There were no handshakes at parting. They went down the steps and walked past the stationary lorry and up the track towards the road. Just as they reached the first bend that would take them out of sight of the house Fletcher glanced back. The man and the woman and the six children were gathered on the veranda, watching them. He gave a wave of the hand, but there was no answering wave. He turned his head and went on with the other two.

" They thought we did it," Lawrence said. " They surely thought we did it."

" Does that surprise you?" Fletcher asked. " In their place wouldn't you have thought so?"

" Mebbe I would."

" The question," King said, " is what will they do about it?"

Fletcher looked at him. " You think they'll do anything?"

" I think it's likely. They'll want to put themselves in the clear; they won't want it to come out that they harboured assassins and did nothing. The man especially. My guess is he'll take that lorry and drive like hell to the nearest police-station or telephone and put in a report. And then they'll be on our tail real fast."

" That's not so funny."

" It's not funny at all. I don't think we should stick to the road for long."

" You know another way?"

" I know another way. It's tough going, but it's safer." King looked at Lawrence. " Think you can make it?"

" I can make it," Lawrence said. " You don't have to worry about me."

" I think you just might at that."

Lawrence certainly looked a lot fitter, and as the sun sank lower it had become less hot; the trees were casting longer shadows and there was a light breeze rattling the leaves.

King had certainly not been exaggerating, however, when he had said it would be tough. There were footpaths of a sort in places, but often there were none; and they had to do a lot of climbing up and down slopes, which was not easy for Lawrence. Nevertheless, he stuck to it without complaint, and King called a halt now and then for rest and recuperation. Fletcher was not sure how badly Lawrence was in need of these breaks, but he knew that he needed them himself. Once they heard the clatter of a helicopter, and quickly took cover. The helicopter flew over fairly low, and it could have been searching for them; but there was no certainty of that. When the sound of it had faded away they went on.

The sun had gone down and the light was rapidly failing when they reached the house. They had approached it from the north side, and they made a slight detour to the left, keeping a sharp lookout for anyone lurking in the grounds. There seemed to be no one; but when they got to the front of the house they saw that their caution had not been entirely unwarranted, for it was at once apparent that Denning had visitors. Two cars were parked on the semi-circle of gravel below the terrace—a Chrysler and a big Citroën.

" Either of you know those cars?" Fletcher asked.

" Not me," Lawrence said.

King did not recognise them, either; but he decided to take a closer look. The cars were backed up against a low stone wall that made a sweeping curve round the edge of the gravel. King crept up to the wall and peered over; and there must have been just enough daylight left to allow him to see inside, for when he rejoined the other two he was able to report that there was no one in either of them.

" No chauffeurs. No spies."

" Do you think they could be police cars?" Fletcher asked.

" They don't look like police cars. And besides, if the police were here there'd be Land-Rovers and God knows what. The place would be crawling with them."

" It's all so damned quiet, too," Lawrence said. " Nothing seems to be going on."

Night was coming swiftly now, and lights were showing in the windows of the house; but there was no sign of any unusual activity within. Yet somehow it was difficult to believe that whoever had arrived in the two cars had come on a purely social call. It was a problem; but it was one that would not be solved by waiting outside; there they were in the dark both figuratively and literally.

" I'm going to investigate," King said. " You two wait here."

Fletcher saw him pat his pocket and guessed that he was reassuring himself that the pistol was still there. He obviously thought he might need it. Fletcher fervently hoped he would not, because if he had to use the gun they were all going to be in real trouble. A moment later he was gone.

Fletcher and Lawrence waited in the shadows. King appeared in the light on the terrace and they saw him go to the door. He did not ring the bell, but apparently the door had not been locked, for he pushed it open and walked in. A very short while had elapsed before he was again in the doorway; and now Denning was with him, so it seemed likely they had met in the entrance hall. King pointed into the darkness, obviously showing Denning where the others were lurking, and Denning turned in that direction and made a beckoning gesture with his hand.

" Well," Lawrence said, " it looks like it's okay. We may as well get over there."

Fletcher had a feeling of relief; he had been afraid there

might be some sticky business, but apparently there was not
to be any; they could relax. The sticky business might well
catch up with them later, but for the present things were
going smoothly; and that was something to be thankful for.
There remained the question of Leonora Dubois, of course;
that would have to be thrashed out and it was not going to
be a pleasant operation, but at least it could be done without violence; there would be no need for guns.

Lawrence went ahead and he followed. They came into
the light and climbed the steps to the terrace. Denning and
King were waiting for them.

" Thank God you're back," Denning said. " You really
had me worried." He noticed Lawrence's bandaged arm.
" What the devil happened to you?"

" I got in the way of a bullet," Lawrence said.

" Oh, that's bad; that really is bad. But things have been
happening all over. You heard about the President?"

" We heard."

" Ah!" Denning was looking past them, as though
searching for someone else. " Where's Leonora?"

" We haven't seen her," King said.

" But she was to pick you up. She took the Ford."

" We came back a different way. It seemed advisable in
the circumstances."

" Oh, I see." Denning seemed to think it over. Then he
said: " Well, there's no point in standing here. Let's go
inside and you can tell me all about it."

They went inside. Fletcher closed the door. Denning
crossed to the door of the big drawing-room, pushed it open
and stood aside for them to go in. They went in and came
to a sudden halt, staring.

" Allow me to introduce you," Denning said. " Though

you, John, I believe, have met these gentlemen before."

"Yes," Fletcher said; "I have."

Sitting on a sofa were the Americans, Frank Hutchins and Dale Brogan. In an armchair, placidly smoking a cigar and seemingly walled in by the arms and the back, was the small dried-up figure of Colonel Arthur W. Vincent of the Jamestown police.

Hutchins's eyes gleamed behind the steel-rimmed glasses and he gave a little flip of the hand. "Hi there, John! Nice to see you again. Still all in one piece, too."

Fletcher's brain was going at the double, trying to work out all the implications while Denning went urbanely through the introduction of King and Lawrence to the other men. Denning seemed perfectly at ease; he did not give the impression of a man who was in any kind of trouble. Yet what else could the presence of Vincent and Hutchins and Brogan indicate but trouble?

Lawrence and King were obviously bewildered and un-easy; trying, like Fletcher, to get the hang of the situation and probably making no better job of it.

Vincent took the cigar out of his mouth, looked at Lawrence, and said: "You appear to have sustained an injury. I trust it is nothing serious."

"No," Lawrence muttered; "nothing serious."

"He was unfortunate enough, so I understand," Denning said, "to stand in the way of a bullet. The circumstances of the incident have not yet been made clear to me, but no doubt we shall all be given an account of it now, since I am sure we are all very much interested. Are you going to tell us, Lawrence? Or is it to be you, Matthew? Or perhaps you, John?"

Fletcher wondered what kind of game Denning was

playing. Did he really expect them to tell what had happened to the C.I.A. men and Colonel Vincent? Or was he inviting them to make up some plausible story on the spur of the moment? If so, he was not getting much response; no one was saying anything.

"Perhaps," Vincent said, puffing out cigar smoke in fragrant clouds, "I might suggest a possible explanation. I have a feeling, Mr. Fletcher, that you have been trying to take some more photographs of a certain boat. I think that, in spite of the friendly warning I gave you a day or two ago, you have again been meddling in matters that are no concern of yours. Is that not so?"

Fletcher said nothing.

"Well," Vincent said, "I'm glad to see you're not going to deny it. You know you really are a most obstinate and troublesome young man. You are aware, I suppose, that there is a warrant out for your arrest on a charge of murder?"

"I've murdered no one," Fletcher said.

"Ah, so you do deny that?"

"Yes."

Vincent shrugged, and seemed to shrug himself deeper into the embrace of the armchair. "It doesn't matter. The men were no great loss. Scum." He gave a snap of the fingers, dismissing them; and Fletcher got the impression that the Colonel had no time for private armies and bodyguards; perhaps believing that they usurped his own position and undermined the authority of the police. "And besides, there are now far more important matters to attend to. The President has been assassinated and the culprits must be brought to justice. That will be done, never fear. Meanwhile, government must go on; affairs of state must be attended to; things cannot be allowed to drift."

Fletcher wondered what all this was leading up to. Colonel Vincent sucked at his cigar and blew more smoke into the air; then said :

" We have to have another president."

" You are going to have an election?" Fletcher asked.

Vincent smiled faintly. Hutchins and Brogan also gave fleeting smiles, as though pitying such naïvety.

Vincent said : " There will be no need to hold an election. We have already chosen the man." He looked at Denning.

Fletcher also looked at Denning. Lawrence and King did the same, staring in disbelief.

" You !" Fletcher said.

Denning nodded. " I have accepted the office."

" But you . . . It's impossible."

" Why impossible?" Denning inquired blandly. " Are you suggesting I am incapable of carrying out the duties of president?"

" You know that's not what I am suggesting."

" What, then?"

" Do you want me to spell it out?"

" If that would be any satisfaction to you, do so by all means."

" Then what about your other activities?"

" Ah," Denning said, " you are talking, of course, about my connections with the revolutionary movement. Now you mustn't run away with the idea that that is any obstacle to the proposed appointment."

" No obstacle !"

" Far from it. Quite the opposite, in fact."

Fletcher glanced at Vincent and the Americans to see what their reactions were. To his amazement they appeared entirely unmoved by this revelation that Denning had been mixed up with revolutionaries. Only King and Lawrence seemed at all affected, and they looked as bewildered as he was himself. He turned again to Denning.

" I don't understand."

" No? Think a little. Why do you suppose this house has always been immune from the attentions of the security forces? Why have I always been free to move about at will? Ah, now I see you are beginning to understand."

He was right. Suddenly the whole thing had become clear to Fletcher. It was Denning who had been the double-dealer; he who had been the source of all the inside information regarding the activities of the guerrilla groups. All the time, while posing as a friend to the revolutionaries, he had in fact been working hand-in-glove with the authorities, with his cousin, Clayton Rodgers. Perhaps he, too, had been on the C.I.A. pay-roll. And perhaps his scheming had been even more Machiavellian still; perhaps he had from the first had his eye on the Presidency and had made full use of his connections on both sides of the political scene to further his ambitions. Perhaps it was he who, when the time seemed ripe, had arranged the killing of President Rodgers, knowing that he would be the one to step into his cousin's shoes. Yes, that was how it had been. That was how it must have been.

And Leonora? Where did she fit into the pattern? As a collaborator with Denning? As a link between him and the C.I.A. rather than as a C.I.A. spy on his activities? It seemed only too probable.

Denning was smiling. " You do understand, don't you?"

" Yes," Fletcher said, " I understand now. I understand how the *Halcón Español* came to be sunk, how five men came to be killed, how the *Freedom* press came to be raided, how it came about that we were anticipated at the wreck today, how Lawrence came to be shot in the arm. I believe I even understand how the President came to be assassinated."

" My cousin Clayton was the wrong man to be Head of State. You must admit that."

Fletcher glanced again at the Americans. " Was that also your opinion?"

Hutchins shrugged. " We have to take the long view."

It was as much as to say that they preferred Conrad Denning to Clayton Rodgers. Perhaps Rodgers had been getting a shade too independent, a little too big for his boots. So he had had to be replaced by a more reliable man. And Colonel Vincent, of course, was only too ready to leap on to any bandwagon that happened to be around. An agile man, the Colonel.

King took a step towards Denning. " You damned traitor!" His right hand made a move for the pistol.

" Hold it there," Brogan said.

There was a stubby revolver in Brogan's hand. Hutchins was holding another. One was pointing at King, one at Lawrence.

King stopped. Lawrence had hardly begun to move. They both looked angry. Fletcher remembered how ruthless they had been with the two Leopards and he was pretty sure that neither of them would have hesitated to kill Denning if it had not been for the revolvers in the hands of the C.I.A. men. He had betrayed them, and they would find that hard to forgive.

Denning himself was perfectly cool. He turned to Vincent and said : " Perhaps you would be good enough to disarm them, Colonel. They are very hot-headed."

Vincent, with the cigar still stuck in his mouth, got up quickly and relieved Lawrence and King of their weapons. He unloaded the pistols, dropped the magazines in his pocket, and laid the guns on a coffee table. He moved on to Fletcher.

" You won't find anything on me," Fletcher said.

Vincent smiled. " Nevertheless . . ."

He did a quick frisking and found nothing. Then he returned to his armchair and continued smoking the cigar.

" What do you intend doing with us?" King asked, staring at Denning with hatred.

Denning looked at him reflectively. Then he said: " I think you will have to come with us."

" Where?"

" To Jamestown. We shall be leaving shortly." Fletcher got the impression that he was simply waiting for Leonora to return, though he could not be sure of that. " There I am afraid it will be necessary to put you under restraint."

" You mean throw us in gaol?"

" Yes."

" And then?"

" You will eventually come up for trial. It will all be done according to the law."

King looked as though he would have liked to spit. " And what are we being charged with?"

" Oh, that is no difficulty. I am sure we can think of something. Treason perhaps. Plotting against the State. Even murder. The choice is wide enough."

" You bet it is."

Fletcher wondered whether he was included with King and Lawrence. It was not a happy thought, for if there was a trial there could be little doubt about the verdict or even the sentence. Denning, having taken over the Presidency, would not be slow to remove as many enemies as possible; and those who had been his closest allies in the revolutionary cause would now be his bitterest opponents.

He became aware that Denning was looking at him.

" Don't you wish you had accepted that offer of two thousand dollars for leaving the island?"

Fletcher glanced at Hutchins. " Would I have got it?"

" Oh, sure," Hutchins said. " It was an honest to God offer. But I'm afraid it's not on any more."

" I didn't think it would be."

" Now," Denning said, " you'll just have to go without any payment; at your own expense."

Fletcher's heart gave a leap. " You mean you're letting me go?"

" Why not? You have committed no offence as far as I am aware. After all, photography is not a crime."

" Or murder?"

Denning dismissed the suggestion with a flutter of the hand. " We know you have not murdered anyone. We know very well who did the killing on the occasion in question. Why, then, should we detain you?"

" Why, indeed."

" I imagine you are not going to make a fuss about going?"

" It would be rather foolish to do that."

" I'm glad you see it in that light. Frankly, I think it would be by far the best way out of the situation."

" I suppose you might say it would be, since you failed to get rid of me the other way."

" The other way? Oh, you're referring to that bit of shooting while you were on board my boat."

" And the underwater explosion while I was down by the wreck. I nearly got caught by that. It was really very nasty, I can tell you. But why should that bother you?"

" Now there," Denning said, " you must believe me when I assure you I would not have had that happen if I could have prevented it. But things had gone too far. I simply couldn't call off the operation."

Fletcher did not believe him. But it made no difference. The main thing was that he was alive and they were going to let him go. He was sorry for King and Lawrence, but they had known what they were doing; they had known that there was always the possibility of being caught, and that if they were they would have to face the consequences. He, on the other hand, had never really been one of them; he had been dragooned into the business. Now he was out of it, and he would be glad to go.

He thought of Leonora and felt a pang, because for a while he certainly had believed that something was building up between them and he had hoped it might go on building; but all of that had come tumbling down and he would just have to forget about it. She was in league with Denning and she must have known very well what was going to happen to him even as she stood on the board-walk and watched the boat leaving harbour. Damn her.

But then he thought again, and there was something that did not quite fit. Denning had said that she had taken the Ford and gone to meet the boat. Yet why should she do that if she had not been expecting them to come back? So maybe she had not known after all. Maybe she had not been working with Denning and the C.I.A. Maybe she was entirely innocent of any betrayal.

The more he thought about it, the more he felt like

buying that. He wanted to believe it, he really did want to believe it, because it threw such a different light on her conduct; and until he had proof that he was wrong he damned well was going to believe it. And of course it explained why Denning was waiting for her : he was waiting so that he could have her arrested the same as King and Lawrence had been arrested; so that she could be thrown in gaol and brought to trial also.

When he had reached that conclusion he began trying to think of a way to prevent its happening. But he had still not come up with any reasonable plan when he heard the crunch of wheels on the gravel outside and then the slam of the car door, and he guessed that Leonora had arrived. He saw Denning stiffen and knew that he was aware of it, too. And if it came to that, he doubted if there was anyone in the room who was not aware of it. He heard her feet on the gravel and then on the terrace, and he could tell that she was running. Then the front door opened and slammed behind her and she was in the hall. He had to stop her now or it would be too late.

He started moving towards the door with a vague intention of heading her off and telling her to turn round, run back to the car and get to hell out of there. It would have been hopeless anyway, because to get her to do that would have taken a lot of explanation and persuasion, and there was just not the time available. But in the event he failed to get even as far as the door, because Brogan jumped up and got between it and him and rammed the muzzle of the revolver into his stomach.

" Stop right there," Brogan said.

Fletcher stopped right there. He had no doubt whatever that Brogan was prepared to use the revolver, and if he provoked him into doing so it was going to help no one, least of all John Fletcher.

A moment later the door burst open and Leonora rushed into the room. She came to an abrupt halt and stared; and it was obvious that her mind was racing, trying to catch up with the situation. It was probable that she recognised Vincent, still sitting in the armchair and placidly smoking his cigar, and it was possible that, even if she did not know them, she guessed who Hutchins and Brogan were; the revolvers were sufficient evidence that they were not there on a purely social visit. But there were details that needed filling in, and she looked at Denning for enlightenment.

" What's going on ?"

" A lot of things are going on," Denning said. " You have perhaps heard that the President has been shot ?"

" Yes. But only a short while ago. That's why I decided to come back and not wait any longer for the boat."

" Just as well. You would have had to wait a long time."

Her head turned towards Fletcher. " What happened?"

" We had trouble," Fletcher said. " There's been a lot of treachery knocking around."

" Treachery !" she said; and he could see that she had known nothing about it. Either that or she was putting on a good act; and he did not believe she was acting. She had not known; and he was glad about that. " What kind of treachery ?"

King suddenly pointed an accusing finger at Denning. " Ask him. He can tell you."

She stared at Denning. " What does he mean?"

Denning gave a slight shrug. " He means, my dear, that I am to be the new president."

" You !" She could not believe it. " It's not possible. Not you."

" Oh, yes," he said; " it is possible. Indeed, I might say it is inevitable."

She seemed utterly bewildered. She glanced at Vincent, as though for confirmation; and Vincent gave a thin smile and a little nod of the head. It seemed to get through to her then. She looked again at Denning and spoke without raising her voice.

" You bastard !" she said. " You filthy, low-down, stinking bastard ! My God, you make me sick !"

FOURTEEN

OF INTEREST

Denning frowned. The girl's contemptuous words had got through to him and touched a nerve. His voice had lost some of its urbanity when he said:

" Let's not have any histrionics; we are dealing with realities. You've been floating around in the clouds long enough; now it's time to come down to earth. This island is never going to be another Cuba; it's not going Red and you'd better accept the fact." His glance took in King and Lawrence. " All of you."

They said nothing; merely stared back at him with hatred in their eyes.

" And now," Denning said briskly, " we have no more time to waste. We must be moving. There's a lot to do."

Colonel Vincent stubbed out his cigar in a convenient ash-tray and stood up. " I am ready."

" Let's go, then."

One of the servants appeared in the hall as they were going out. Denning snapped a curt order and the man retired hurriedly after giving one frightened glance at the guns Hutchins and Brogan were carrying. The light from the terrace was shining across the gravelled space below, revealing the Ford in which Leonora had arrived, and the

Citroën and the Chrysler backed up against the low peri-
meter wall. They went down the steps and walked across to
them, Hutchins and Brogan keeping close to King and
Lawrence to make sure they did not attempt to break
away.

" Leave the Ford," Denning said. " We'll use the other
two cars."

Brogan directed King to get into the front passenger seat
of the Chrysler, while Hutchins and Lawrence climbed into
the back. Brogan pocketed his revolver and got in behind
the wheel. At the same time the others were piling into the
Citroën, Vincent in the driving seat with Fletcher beside
him; Denning and the girl in the back.

That was when the three men came over the wall. They
must have been watching from the shadows and had probably guessed something of what was going on, if not all.
Fletcher caught sight of them at the same moment as
Brogan and Hutchins must have done. He saw the doors of
the Chrysler swing open and Brogan step out on one side
and Hutchins on the other. Brogan had his revolver in his
hand again, and Hutchins had never put his away. Not that
the weapons were going to be any use to them, because the
men who had come over the wall were carrying submachine-
guns and they were not waiting for anyone else to start the
shooting; they started it themselves.

Hutchins and Brogan were so close to the blast of the
guns that they seemed to be blown backwards. Fletcher
ducked below the dashboard then and lost sight of them,
because he had seen the third man coming towards the
Citroën holding his own submachine-gun at the ready. And
suddenly Vincent's nerve cracked; he opened the car door
and made a run for it. Fletcher lost sight of him also, but he

heard the brief stutter of the gun and guessed that Vincent had not got very far.

Everything went very quiet after that, and a few seconds later he lifted his head cautiously and saw Vincent lying face downward on the gravel about ten yards away. The man who had shot him was standing over him and looking down. And then he rolled the body over with his foot and looked at the face, and gave a short, sharp laugh and turned away.

King was getting out of the Chrysler, stepping carefully over Brogan's body. He walked over to the Citroën and looked in and said :

" Better go back to the house now. Looks like there's been a change of plan."

*   *   *

They were all big men; so big that the submachine-guns in their hands looked like toys. One of them was coffee-coloured and pock-marked, and he had a dirty rag of a bandage on his right forearm. The blood had run down on to his hand and had not been washed off but had simply been allowed to dry on the skin. The other two were as black as coal, and they all looked tired and dusty and as hard as rocks. Fletcher did not need to be told where they had come from or what they had been doing; nobody did. He wondered which one had shot the President, or whether each of them had put a bullet or two into the tyrant, sharing the blood between them like the assassins of Julius Caesar.

They sat on the chairs in Denning's drawing-room and their eyes looked dull with fatigue. None of the servants had put in an appearance, though they must have heard the shooting; they were keeping their heads down, and Fletcher did not blame them. King had explained briefly to the three men just what the situation was. They had looked at Denning with death in their faces, but he had stared back at them coldly, without flinching, faintly contemptuous.

King said to him : " You will come with us now."

" For what purpose?" Denning asked. " To be killed? I would rather be shot here."

" To be tried."

" It is the same thing."

King shrugged. " You may think so."

He did not discuss the matter further, but turned to Fletcher. " What will you do?"

" My plans haven't changed. I shall still leave the island."

" That may not be so easy now. If you went to Jamestown and tried to board an airliner or a ship I think you would be arrested. Who is there to vouch for you now?"

Fletcher appreciated the difficulty. The warrant for his arrest still stood, and now there were other incidents in which he had been involved. There could be little doubt that if he attempted to leave the island by the regular means he would inevitably end up in gaol.

" What do you suggest?"

" You could join us," King said.

There was little attraction in that alternative. Joining King and his comrades would mean taking to the hills, the guerrilla hideouts; it would mean being on the run, hunted by the security forces, winkled out of one foxhole after another; it would mean living rough and being always in danger. And for what? An ideal in which he had no belief.

"No," he said; "I don't think that's the game for me. There must be some way of getting off the island."

"There's the boat," King said.

Fletcher glanced at Denning, who gave a sardonic laugh. "If you are asking my permission, take it. It's hardly likely that I shall ever have need of it again. Charon's boat is the only one I shall use."

Fletcher shook his head. "I should never find my way back to it."

"That's true," King admitted. "You would need a guide." He seemed to think about it; then he said: "Very well; I will take you back to the boat."

"I'll go with you," Leonora said.

Fletcher and King looked at her, but neither of them made any remark.

*   *   *

They travelled the first part of the journey in the Ford. King said it would bring them closer to the boat before they had to go on foot. None of them was going back to the house; when King had seen Fletcher safely to the boat he would make his own way to join up with the other party at a prearranged rendezvous. What Leonora proposed doing neither of them knew. She had packed a duffle-bag but had given no hint regarding her plans; perhaps had not even made up her own mind. Fletcher had abandoned his suit-case and had brought only the canvas holdall. They had all eaten a hurried meal before leaving and had brought some extra provisions with them. King said there were some reserve cans of petrol in the boat and still a useful amount in the tanks.

" You'll have enough. All you have to do is head west and you're bound to hit land pretty soon."

Fletcher was not so sure about that; there was a lot more water than land and it would be rough navigation at best. But he preferred to take that risk rather than the risk of going with the guerrillas or trying to get away by the orthodox method; the police in Jamestown were likely to be very vigilant, and anyone who might have had any connection with the assassination of President Rodgers or the killing of Colonel Vincent was not going to find it easy to slip through their fingers.

The boat was in the place where it had been left and there was no indication that anyone had tampered with it. They had left the Ford some four miles back and Fletcher knew that he would never have found the way without King. There was a thin sliver of moon, but by the time they reached the boat it was low in the sky. There was just enough light to reveal where the controls were.

" You think you can handle it?" King asked.

" I think so," Fletcher said. He had had some lessons from Joby in boat-handling and he had seen Lawrence working this one. It was simple enough.

" Okay then," King said. " She's all yours."

He was referring to the boat, but Fletcher was looking at the girl. Leonora had not stepped on board; she was standing a few yards away with the duffle-bag slung over her right shoulder.

" Are you coming with me?" he asked.

She turned her head and looked at King, as though seeking his advice.

King said : " You please yourself. If you want to go with him, you go."

"Don't you want me to stay with you? Isn't that what you really want?"

"Sure, that's what I want. Nothing I want more. You know that. But it's for you to choose."

Fletcher waited, not saying anything. She took a step towards the boat and he thought she had decided to go with him, and his heart leaped. But then she stopped.

"You see how it is, John. I can't leave him now. I owe him that much. You must understand."

"I understand," Fletcher said. "I love you, but I understand. You have to do what you have to do."

He began tinkering with the controls. The engine came to life. King cast off the mooring-rope.

"Goodbye," King said.

Fletcher had the boat moving then. He took it out into the middle of the creek and headed for the sea, not looking back. He had come to where the creek widened out when he slowed and turned the boat and went back. They were still standing where he had left them, almost as though they had expected him to return. He brought the boat in close to the bank and stopped the engine and threw the rope to King. He picked up his holdall and tossed it on to the bank and jumped after it.

"You changed your mind," King said. He sounded unsurprised. He might have been anticipating it.

"Yes, I changed my mind. I'm coming with you."

"Why?"

"I got to feeling lonely," Fletcher said. "There's an awful lot of sea out there and I'm no navigator. A man needs friends."

King nodded. "That's true."

"Maybe more than friends," Leonora said.

Her voice was husky and it sounded like a promise of some kind. Fletcher had a feeling she was glad he had come back, and he knew that he himself was.

" Maybe so," he said. " Maybe so at that."

*   *   *

They had been travelling for about an hour with King in the lead, followed by Leonora, and Fletcher bringing up the rear, when the girl slowed down to allow him to draw level with her.

" What was that you said just before you started the boat?" she asked. " I've been trying to remember."

Fletcher cast his mind back a little. " I said you have to do what you have to do."

" No, not that. There was something else. I'm sure there was something else."

" I said I love you."

" Yes, that's it," she said. " I thought that was what you said."

She went on ahead again, but a little later she was back at his side. " If it's of any interest to you," she said, " I love you, too."

" It is of interest," Fletcher said.